Beyond the
Shallow Bank

David A. Wimsett

BEYOND THE SHALLOW BANK
Cape Split Press
http://www.capesplitpress.com

An imprint off Your Story 2 video Ltd.

TM

Published by arrangement with the author

The characters and events in this book are fictitious. Any similarity to real persons, living or dead, is coincidental and unintended by the author

PRINTING HISTORY
Second Paperback Edition / December 2017

ISBN: 978-1-7750890-4-9

Printed in the Unites States of America

ACKNOWLEDGEMENTS

There are many people who have helped me bring this book to life. My editor, Nancy Cassidy, worked with me to hone the writing and make it shine. Four wonderful woman, Karen, Laura, Lisa and Ann, all read versions of the manuscript and gave invaluable feedback on the perspective of woman. Karen and Lisa shared intimate details about their birth stories. There are also the members of Leonard Bishop's weekly writing group. Leonard taught me the nuts and bolts of writing that allowed me to turn ideas into stories. Finally, I thank the many staff and participants at the Squaw Valley Community of Writers Workshops where I learned to polish my craft.

David A. Wimsett
Nova Scotia
2017

Dedicated to the memory my parents,
Margaret and John Wimsett

Beyond the

Shallow Bank

PROLOGUE

New York
April, 1899

The oil lamp on the bedside table was turned down such that it cast more shadow than light. Margaret Talbot lay for an instant and panted as she stared up at the ceiling. Then the pain returned, like dozens of razors ripping through her. Margaret arched her back and muffled a scream.

The midwife leaned down and wiped sweat from Margaret's forehead before standing to make the sign of the cross. Margaret cried out, "John."

The door opened and her husband ran in to kneel at her bedside. His moustache was untrimmed and his hair was tousled. He took her hand in his and held it against his cheek. "I've hailed a carriage. We'll be at the hospital in a few minutes."

"Something's wrong."

He kissed her hand gently. "The doctor said labor could be hard with a first child."

"Not like this. Something's wrong. I can feel it."

John held her hand until the driver arrived to help carry Margaret downstairs. The pain came in stabbing waves. She tried to concentrate on the tulip and willow wallpaper, the paintings and sculptures they had collected from around the world, the stained glass window John had commissioned when they first learned she was with child—anything but her body.

She had to sit up in the carriage as it bounced along the cobblestone streets and the driver urged the two horses into a gallop. At the hospital, Margaret was moved to a wheeled cot and rushed down a corridor by a male orderly. He wore a white coat splattered with reddish-brown stains. Her vision blurred and she thought she might faint.

The cot burst through a swinging door into a narrow room. Bare electric bulbs hung down from wires overhead. Doctors and nurses wearing white masks over their mouths and noses gathered around her. The orderly wheeled her beneath a light with a reflector behind it. Her legs were raised into metal stirrups. A buzz of voices echoed around the room.

She clenched her teeth as a contraction gripped her. A nurse said, "The patient is ready, Doctor."

"Forceps."

"Here comes the head."

"Ready."

"There it is."

"I've got it."

Margaret's fingers tingled, but she could no longer feel her legs.

A nurse said, "Doctor, I have no heartbeat."

"Can you get a breath?"

Margaret started to sit up as nausea nearly overcame her. "What's happened to my baby? Is it a boy or a girl? Let me see."

A firm hand pressed her down. "Relax, dear," said one of the nurses loudly. "Everything is going to be just fine." The nurse continued to hold her down as she heard another one whisper, "Doctor, it's a stillbirth."

"Dead? Dump it over there and help me with the mother. I can't stop this bleeding."

It was a horrible dream, Margaret decided. She would wake up in a moment and John would put his arms around her and push the nightmare away.

"Clamp."

"Clamp."

"Suture. Someone wipe that blood away so I can see."

"Doctor, I'm losing her pulse."

"Mrs. Talbot, can you hear me? Mrs. Talbot. Do you want a priest?"

It seemed her head was floating above her and she fought to make sense of the words. Still, the doctor's tone filled her with terror. "Where is my husband?"

She turned her head and saw John charge through the swinging door. An orderly appeared from behind and grabbed him. The voices in the room were mumbles in Margaret's ears. The doctor spoke with John, who gestured wildly. Another orderly arrived. The doctor spoke again. John looked to Margaret with his mouth open as though he were about to scream.

Margaret had the vague feeling that there was something important she had to tell him, but the more she tried to remember, the further the memory retreated.

The orderlies dragged John back through the door. People ran around her frantically, now. It had all become a pantomime; the shouts and orders collected together into a droning roar.

She closed her eyes and the drone took on a rhythm, loud and soft, high and low, the pounding of the surf on a distant beach. She imagined herself standing there, alone except for the sea and the waves that drew ever closer.

CHAPTER ONE

The eastern shore of Nova Scotia, Canada
August, 1901

The dirt road was level now and the horse-drawn wagon carrying Margaret and John made good time on its way to the fishing village of Glasen. Margaret consulted the nurse's watch she kept pinned to her jacket. It was two hours before noon and the air was already hot and humid.

John sat on the far end of a padded bench reading a copy of the English magazine, *Fortnightly Review*. He had been studying it all morning without a single word to Margaret. This was business. That was all that held them together now.

John lowered the magazine. "You're very quiet today."

A chill shook her, even in the hot summer air. John's dark brown eyes stared into hers. She imagined him crawling into her head and seeing the secret thoughts hidden there. She reached down to the floor of the wagon and retrieved a sketchbook and a pencil. She began drawing little circles and arcs on the pad. "I was thinking of what to illustrate next. Eight weeks isn't much time."

John returned to the magazine. "We've met worse deadlines. We'll make this one."

Did he know she was thinking of leaving him? It would not be easy. Divorce wasn't legal in New York. Margaret's friend Edith had traveled to Mexico to obtain one. When Edith had returned to New York, her commissions had dried up. The galleries turned down her work. She was no longer invited to parties. She stayed with an aunt, not her mother. One day, Edith just wasn't there anymore. Margaret hadn't heard from her in years.

As she had so many times before, she considered returning alone to the New Jersey farm where she'd been born. John probably wouldn't care. It wasn't as if they were really married. Not as man and wife; not since *the incident*.

It was something neither of them spoke of. Where once they had fallen asleep in each other's arms, now they slept in separate rooms. Margaret knew her socialite friends would find nothing strange in this. Indeed, they had always considered her and John to be quaint but somewhat odd for their displays of affection. There were no longer any such displays.

When she'd awakened in the hospital, drained and frightened, she'd feebly reached her hand out to John. He'd stared at it, as though trying to make out what it was, then looked to the doctor standing next to him before stepping back from Margaret's side. From that moment, John had cut off all physical contact with her.

He'd given no reason. He didn't even acknowledge the change. Margaret wasn't certain if he blamed her for their child's death or if he had just grown tired of her.

She studied him now. At thirty-six, he was five years older than her. His skin was tanned and slightly cracked from years in the sun. His dark hair, so unlike her blond tresses, was combed straight back. He wore a neatly-trimmed moustache that used to brush softly against her skin the instant before they kissed. She forced down the memory deep within

5

her.

She shifted back to her professional illustrator persona and ignored the voices clawing inside her. There was a magazine article to create, as they had created so many others over the past decade. She did not have the luxury of indulging in distracting thoughts.

She started by sketching the wagon driver, James Duncan, who sat on a bench in front of them. Margaret judged him to be nearly fifty, a stocky man, short with graying hair. The wagon had two benches and a bed in the rear. It was lacquer black with red spoked wheels. Duncan held the reins loosely in his hands, guiding the single chestnut horse that pulled the wagon. Having grown up on a farm near the sea, Margaret was certain the horse knew the road so well by now that it could make the journey by itself.

The wagon plodded through a forest so dense she could see no more than a few feet into the woods. It spread in all directions, broken only by streams, rivers and lakes that would appear suddenly through the foliage. Oak and spruce and ash and pine and sugar maple formed a patchwork of varying green hues that splashed across the canopy in a spectrum running from yellowish-green to deep emerald. Standing in stark contrast were the trunks of the birches, their light bark peeling in horizontal curls. Directly above was a bright blue sky with fluffy clouds.

Margaret sketched the woods. While she worked, she made notes on the side to describe the colors. The notes and sketches were quick impressions, frameworks for illustrations to be completed later in ink.

"John, what hue would you say the leaves of that birch are?"

He looked up from the magazine. Sweat had formed on his forehead just below the band of the motoring cap he wore along with a tweed coat neatly buttoned up to his starched collar, even though it was sweltering. The wagon rolled on for a moment before he set his magazine down. "Why do you ask?"

"For the illustrations in the article."

He looked at the forest and back to her. "Every illustration you have ever drawn has been in black ink on white paper."

"Well, perhaps I'd like to work in color."

"Pen and ink is our trademark. Everyone expects it."

"Did you ever consider that I might want to produce something other than an illustration? Maybe I want to do a painting."

John ignored her and returned to his magazine.

She drew circles on the side of the sketchbook. "A few paintings would be nice for that lecture series you want to give."

John closed his eyes and took a deep breath. "How many times do we have to have this discussion?"

She flung her sketchbook to the floor of the wagon. "Why don't you just say it? You've never wanted me to paint."

"Where did you get such an idea?"

"Where do you think? Every time I mention painting you have some excuse why I can't. 'We have a deadline.' 'The ship's about to sail.' Always some subtle reason. Well, you're not so subtle when you think I'm not around."

"I don't know what you're talking about."

"You thought I was in another room at that party last month when you told James Fredrick I had no talent for oils. Remember? *I* do, and God knows who else does."

"I said you were not practiced in oils, as in, you had not practiced in a while. Why do you read something extra into everything I say?"

"Because you put it there." She bent over, retrieved her sketchbook and started to drawing arcs again. "All I want is some time away from the articles. Is that so much to ask?"

John fanned himself with the magazine. "At the moment, we're celebrities. Editors buy our material at premium prices and people read them religiously because we produce a new one while they're still thinking about the last."

"Don't you think I know that? I'm only asking for eighteen months. That will let me finish my studies with Robert Henri. He's living in New York now and taking on selected students for private instruction."

John made a cutting motion with his hand. "I'm not talking about this anymore."

"When you asked me to marry you, I told you I wanted to paint, and you promised the articles would end in five years. Five years and I could return to painting full time. I made that bargain happily, but there wasn't a day I didn't think about working in oils.

"Then, when the time came to stop, you asked me to help finish the articles we had already planned. 'Just a little while longer,' you said, 'and we can leave a completed legacy.'"

John fanned himself more vigorously. "Yes, I know what I said."

She shook her head slowly. "No, John. You don't know. If you did, we wouldn't be having this conversation. Either you've forgotten or you hoped I would. Well, I didn't, and if truth be known I never wanted to complete any of those articles. I wanted to paint, but I put that aside once more because you asked me to. That 'little while' has become two years and there's still no end in sight. I've waited seven years, John. I'm tired of waiting!"

John tried to whisper through clenched teeth. "This is not the time or place to talk about it."

"It is never the time or place."

John twisted the magazine in his hands. "And just where is the money going to come from?"

"Don't treat me like a child. We have savings."

"For our old age."

A dull ache grew behind her right eye as it often did with these discussions. "We are not destitute. If you're so worried about money, write some articles without my illustrations."

A look of fear seemed to cross John's face in that instant. It was gone before she was certain.

He said, "We have a system that works. You'd agreed that it would be my decision as to when we had enough money to stop."

"After five years."

"After however long it takes."

A cloud rolled in from the sea and blocked out the sun. She turned her head to the side. "There's a hole inside me, John, and I'm terrified. I have to be an artist and I'm running out of time."

John's voice softened. "Margaret, you are an artist, a great artist.

I've lost count of the dinners that have been given in your honor, and you've earned each one."

"They were just dinners."

"They were telling you that you are the best, and you are. How many people have been given awards, *medals*, from both publishers and universities? Only you. You're recognized at parties. People love your work."

She dabbed her eyes with a linen handkerchief. "They're just illustrations, not legitimate art."

"What's legitimate?"

"You know what I mean. Renoir is legitimate. And Monet."

"More people have seen your work than both of them combined."

"It's not the same."

"How?"

She looked up to a sky that swirled with gray clouds. "It's like the difference between writing magazine articles and poetry."

John's posture grew rigid. "Are you saying I'm not a real writer because I don't write poetry?"

"I'm saying there's a difference between a magazine illustration and a painting."

"So, let me see if I understand this. You won't accept a compliment for your illustrations because magazine work simply isn't up to your standards, and everyone who writes for a magazine, like me, is just a hack."

"You're not listening to me again."

"Oh, I think I've heard enough." He raised the magazine in front of his face.

Margaret felt her forehead flush hot as she grabbed the periodical out of his hands. "Don't you dare cut me off like that." She threw the magazine out onto the road.

John stared at her before leaning forward. "Mr. Duncan, please stop the wagon."

"No," said Margaret. "Keep driving."

John looked back to her. "Are you mad? Mr. Duncan, stop."

"Keep driving."

Duncan pulled on the reins. "I'm sorry, ma'am, but it be your husband who hired me and it's his order I must follow."

John gave Margaret a short stare before walking back down the road.

Margaret leaned forward. "Drive on. Quickly."

"I dunna' think I can do that ma'am."

"It's all right. The walk will cool him off."

John returned and climbed back on the wagon. Margaret immediately stood up and climbed down to the road. She wasn't sure why she had done so or what she was going to do next. It simply felt like a victory.

James Duncan remained motionless. John said, "What are you doing?"

"I'm sitting up front. You don't mind, do you, Mr. Duncan?"

"Well, ma'am, it's just…"

John waved a hand in the air. "If you want to sit in front go ahead. Perhaps we can reach Glasen in peace."

She climbed up next to Duncan and immediately regretted her decision. The bench she had been sitting on was softly padded and covered in leather. The driver's seat was hard wood. She squirmed uncomfortably for an instant, too prideful to return to the rear bench.

As the wagon moved forward the whole fight seemed so pointless. They couldn't even talk about the color of leaves. What hope was there? There certainly wasn't love anymore.

When she had been very young, her grandmother had told her of a magic spell that would make a husband love his wife again. *"It comes from the sea, Margaret,"* her grandmother had said, *"where all magic lies."* Together, they had spent an hour carefully selecting seashells. In her grandmother's bedroom, they arranged them on the top of a dresser, spreading sand to connect them. Then, her grandmother had sung a song whose words were nonsense, but whose tune Margaret still remembered.

Even as a child, Margaret had not believed in magic. Real

problems didn't vanish just because she wanted them to. Sometimes, it felt as if nothing would make them go away.

It's time to leave, she told herself. *As soon as this article is done*. She picked up the sketchbook and touched the pencil to it, but was unable to draw either arcs or circles.

The wagon skirted the forest to run along a gravel beach. One wheel dropped into a jarring rut and Margaret's charcoal pencil slashed across the paper. James Duncan said, "Sorry. It be a rough ride here and abou'. There's li'l traffic and they'll not spare time to fix the road till it washes out. Seems we ne'er ken the worth o' water till the well be dry."

Margaret had grown accustomed to his Scots burr, but still had to listen intently.

She flipped over a new sheet of paper and looked east. The Atlantic waters could be glimpsed past the openings of small coves and around offshore islands. Gentle waves lapped against the shore, the full force of the ocean contained by the natural barriers. Thin stalks of eelgrass bobbed on the surface of the water and undulated rhythmically beneath. Still more of it lay washed up on the beach, dry and fragile, like shreds of green paper.

She thought about her family's farm near the shore. Since she had been a small child, Margaret had always felt uneasy when she was away from the sea for too long. The sight of the Atlantic filled her with a quiet comfort.

They came to low bluffs of crumbling shale and sandstone that rose above the shoreline. The wagon left the ocean and climbed into thick woods again. The hillside rose steeply to the left and then fell more moderately to the right. Above, a vaulting ceiling of branches nearly cut off the gray sky. Birds fluttered from branch to branch, their songs competing with the clinking tack of the horse.

She and John had spent years planning the current article. It would examine the turn of the twentieth century, contrasting its reception in their urban, New York home with its coming in a rural fishing village.

Margaret's wide-brimmed hat, secured with a lace ribbon beneath her chin, offered some shade from the sun when it peeked in and out of rolling clouds. It brought no relief from the warm, cloying dampness. The long sleeves and high collar of her blouse stuck uncomfortably to her skin. The heat was made worse by her blue, waist-length coat and a thick, ankle-length skirt.

There was a break in the trees and she could see the ocean again. She spied the dual masts and billowing sails of a schooner. This was how most people traveled to out ports like Glasen, all in a day's voyage. Both she and John felt the article would have more impact if they saw the land and stopped at other villages. It was their way—to immerse themselves in their subjects, and they had done so in locations ranging from the arid landscape of the Mojave Desert to the lumber camps of British Columbia; from the steppes of Russia to the savannahs of Africa.

The heat and humidity intensified. Margaret reached up to the collar button of her blouse, hoping not to shock James Duncan by undoing it. At that moment, the air lightened as the clouds overhead formed into dark masses. With no warning, rain poured from the sky. She lifted her head and opened her mouth as droplets flowed down her face and drenched her garments.

Closing her eyes, she recalled standing in the rain as a child, the youngest of eight, and having her eldest brother, Jake, lift her up so she could reach her arms out and try to touch the clouds.

She felt the sketchbook in her hand and opened her eyes with a start. The pages were wet, though the charcoal images were still intact. Laughing, she raised herself off the seat, placed the book beneath her, and sat down to protect it, noticing James Duncan silently watching from the corner of his eye.

Within a few minutes, the rain stopped, leaving the air cleansed of the horrific heat. She breathed in the earthy fragrance. A cool breeze came up from the east and a shiver ran through her. She wanted to ask John to pass up her shawl from the wagon bed, but was still too angry to speak with him.

She said, "Have you ever been to Glasen, Mr. Duncan?"

"Aye, ma'am. I travel through several times a year."

"We're staying at the Glasen Hotel."

"A fine place. Built a year ago. All brick, it is, so's it won't burn down like the last one. There's steam heat and hot water right out o' the wall. It's a wonder to behold."

In their first meeting at the port of Halifax she had asked him if everyone in Nova Scotia spoke with an accent.

He had smiled, "Well now, we could say it's you what's got the accent and we here speak normal."

Margaret remembered blushing.

Duncan had given a laugh. "I take no offense, Ma'am, and intend none. It be a matter of perspective. Now, as to your question, I'm a Lowlander from the south of Scotland, near Paisley. I came across but eight year' ago. You won't hear much Auld Scots in Glasen. It were the people of the Highlands what settled there." He had begun loading their trunks into his wagon even before they had officially hired him. "You'll hear the Gaelic," he had said, "even when they speak English."

Margaret settled back into the wagon bench as comfortably as possible and watched the trees move slowly past. She imagined herself luxuriating at the Glasen Hotel while sitting in a warm tub with scented bath oils. After riding camels in Egypt, living in tents on the Serengeti, and trudging through mud in Argentina, Glasen sounded like a very pleasant assignment.

They reached a wide, grassy meadow where a picket fence enclosed a garden with potatoes, turnips, and carrots planted in neat rows. Next to it was a house whose base was nearly square. From the front it appeared to be a single-story building with a high-pitched roof, but on the gable end was a second story window where Margaret knew a bedroom would be found. She had seen this type of structure as they traveled along the coast. Everyone referred to them as *salt-boxes*.

The house stood atop a low bluff that overlooked the ocean. The clapboard siding was white and the windows were highlighted in dark green trim. Rising above the wood-shingled roof was a stone chimney from which smoke poured across the darkened sky. A ladder next to the chimney hung down from the peak of the roof to the eaves and Margaret knew this was to allow quick access to the chimney if there was a fire in the flue.

At the edge of the bluff was the top landing of stairs that she assumed ran down to a beach. A lithe-framed woman watched the ocean from the landing. Margaret felt certain she was no older than twenty. The young woman wore a skirt and blouse with a shawl wrapped over her brown hair. The shawl's ends whipped wildly in the wind and Margaret would not have been surprised to see the woman's small body knocked over.

"Do you know who that is, Mr. Duncan?"

"That be Sara, wife of Ian Grant. Ian fishes the waters in his small dory, fair or foul. When a storm brews up a' sudden you'll find Sara out there waitin' for him. If you're to write a story on Glasen you'll hear plenty abou' her."

"Why is that?"

He pulled on the reins to bring the horse back to the center of the road. "Five year ago, Ian rowed off in his fishin' dory as he did every day, but he didn't return that evening. His house stood empty for a week and more than a few thought he had drowned. Then, there he was rowin' into Glasen with Sara in the boat. He said he had taken her as wife in his travels."

"Where does she come from?"

"Neither she nor Ian has ever said. All I know is it must be very different from here. The first time I spoke with her, she looks at my horse and asks what it is. So I says, 'Don't you have horses where you come from?' And she says the queerest thing. She says, 'They'd have nowhere to stand.'

"Then, she reaches up and puts her hand on the old mare's cheek. Now, that were a horse what did not abide human company and would as soon bite your fingers off as look at you. But, Sara says somthin' to her—I din'a catch what it was—and that horse nuzzles up to her as tame as a kitten."

"Some people just have a way with animals, Mr. Duncan."

"True enough, ma'am. Still, from then on, that nasty old mare was the kindest animal you could ever want."

Margaret studied the young woman standing at the bluff, caught between the press of the land and the darkening storm clouds above the sea. She felt a sense of kinship with this stranger that she was unable to explain.

Sara turned and looked directly at her. Margaret found she could not pull her gaze away. The young woman stood bright against the dark sky. Margaret imagined the sound of waves mixed with one of the nonsense songs her grandmother used to sing about waves and kelp, though she could never remember how it ended.

The lure of Sara's image intensified. The sky dimmed. All Margaret could concentrate on was Sara's eyes. Margaret began to pant. The sound of the horse's tack was muffled, and all the while Sara's image grew brighter.

Then, Sara blinked and turned away to stare once more out to sea. The contact broken, Margaret shook as a chill ran down her back and legs. Her throat tightened and she nearly fainted.

John leaned forward, his voice alarmed. "Margaret, what's wrong? Are you ill?"

Her voice came dry and hoarse. "Water."

James Duncan stopped the wagon and pressed a canteen into Margaret's hands. She took a deep drink.

John said, "Mr. Duncan, how far are we from Glasen?"

"We're nearly there."

"Please help me move the trunks in the bed so Mrs. Talbot can lie down."

"Aye, sir."

"Then drive us directly to the doctor."

Margaret felt her airway clear. She took in a long, deep breath as she set the canteen on her lap. "It's all right, John. I'm fine now." She was still shaking, unable to either describe or explain what had happened. She convinced herself that she was just upset with John and that James Duncan's story had reminded her of her grandmother and the sea. The strain of the horrible decision to leave John had exhausted her, she told herself.

There was worry in John's eyes as he studied her.

"Are you certain you're all right?" he asked. "It wouldn't take a moment to fix the bed."

She found herself smiling. "I really do feel much better. Thank you."

"At least come sit back here where it's more comfortable."

She nodded and returned to the padded bench.

The very fact that John showed concern had calmed her. It was another glimpse of the man she had met and married, and made thoughts of leaving him difficult. At the same time, a cold sadness settled in her chest as his concern reminded her of how rare such moments were now, and of just how much she had lost.

The wind died down just after five o'clock. They rounded a bend and descended into the fishing village of Glasen. It lay nestled in a valley that opened onto a small harbor. The dirt road ran along its south shore, where houses were built on piers. Across the water, on the north side, was a long wharf on which stood several large buildings made of brick and wood.

Dozens of small boats and a single schooner floated on water so calm it left only ripples against their hulls. Margaret stared in fascination as men stood in the boats, hooked fish with long, barbed poles, and hoisted them up onto the wharf. She made quick sketches as men, women and children took the fish, cut off the heads, split them along the belly, gutted them, and hung the flesh from rungs on racks that looked like stacked cloths lines. Others took fish on a different rack and stacked them in wooden barrels. When a layer was complete coarse salt was sprinkled over them. Men lifted full barrels and hauled them into the buildings. A dull rumble of voices floated on the water, punctuated by the screech of gulls.

They passed two men at the edge of the dock. One sat on a stool while the other took a pipe from his pocket.

The man on the stool said, "*Bha grain ann mu thuath.*"

The other lit his pipe. "*Bidh sìde mhath a dhìth oirnn a-màireach.*"

The first man looked up. "*Cò iad?*"

The other turned around. *"Chan eil mi à tuigsinn."*

Margaret said, "Is that Gaelic, Mr. Duncan?"

"Aye, ma'am."

"What are they saying?"

"They're jus' discussin' the weather, and you."

The wagon moved away from the wharf's din and into the village. She heard the jingle of a bell as a young boy came out of a shop with two small parcels tucked under one arm. Across the street was a dry goods store with a sign reading *Lamont Bros.* Inside, three women stood before a counter. John had been corresponding with a Phillip Lamont. Next door, a blacksmith pumped the hand bellows of his forge as sweat glistened on his muscular arms. A sense of excitement grew in her as she began to plan what she would sketch for the article.

At the end of the street, a white church steeple stood tall above the other buildings. Margaret looked for signs of the Glasen Hotel.

Side streets led off to the left and right with more salt-box houses painted white and green and brown and gray. Some had one or two dormers jutting from the high-peaked roofs and some just second story windows at the gable ends. Many sprouted additions on the backs, sides, or both.

Although thick forests surrounded Glasen, only a handful of trees—mostly maples and elms—stood inside the village itself. The sounds of children playing filled the air. She laughed when someone's mother shouted "You'd best be home 'afore I count t' three."

James Duncan pulled on the reins when they reached a watering trough in front of the post office which shared its wooden building with a printer's shop. "The horse be needin' water, sir, and I hope you don't mind if I take a moment to deliver these here parcels."

John asked, "Is the hotel nearby?"

"Right close, sir. I won't be but a minute."

As they had proceeded up the coast, Margaret discovered that a minute in the Maritimes could mean many things. One did not simply drop off or pick up goods. A certain amount of socializing always took place. *How is the weather? Did your uncle's leg heal? Angus sure seemed sweet on Fiona after church.* Her life in New York was so brisk. Her friends would never be able to stand the gentler pace of life. "I think I'll just stretch my legs," she ventured.

John continued reading. "We're almost at the hotel."

"I'll be back in a minute."

She got down from the wagon, tucked the sketchbook under one arm and slid a pencil into the pocket she had sewn into her skirt, wondering, as she had many times before, why women's garments were not designed with such a useful feature.

During the last decade, Margaret and John had traveled to many small towns around the world for their articles. Often, they had been greeted with suspicion and fear.

So far, John had dealt with the local merchants on this trip. They had seemed pleasant to Margaret, even friendly. But she knew from experience that how innkeepers treated travelers, who were their life blood, was often very different from how the local population treated strangers who asked questions.

She stepped into the Lamont Brothers' store. A young man stood behind the counter, wrapping a package in brown paper. He tied it with a string that came from a metal ball on the counter, fed up through a loop in the ceiling, and came back down to the counter again.

She said, "Excuse me, Mr. Lamont?"

The man looked up. "No, ma'am. I'm their clerk, Angus MacLeod. Neither of the brothers is in today. Alistair Lamont, now he don't come to the store much anymore. Phillip Lamont runs things, but as I said, he's not here today. Can I help you?"

The young man's speech lacked James Duncan's burr, yet still flowed with a musical lilt. He smiled broadly and Margaret found herself smiling back. "My husband and I have been corresponding with Mr. Phillip Lamont and I was just curious to meet him. I understand he is the local magistrate as well as the proprietor."

MacLeod's eyes widened. "You're Mrs. Talbot, aren't you? Mr. Lamont has been talkin' up a storm over your visit. I'm sure glad to meet you, ma'am. We got your latest article right here for sale in the store.

You're really goin' to be makin' a story on us, are you?"

"Yes. We'll be staying into September and speaking with everyone we can."

Two middle-aged women stood a pace away. One wore a green skirt with a brown jacket. The other had a white bonnet with lace trim.

The woman with the green skirt said, "You like makin' magazine articles, do you?"

Like MacLeod, the woman's speech carried a sing-song rhythm. Margaret wasn't certain if this was a question or a challenge, but she smiled anyway. "It's our business."

"I read the one o'er there," said the woman with the bonnet. She pointed to copies of *The Wide World Magazine* sitting on the wooden counter. "Did you really travel to China?"

Margaret tried to gauge the women, but their neutral expressions told her nothing. "We have traveled around the world many times."

The woman shook her head. "I never heard tell of such things before. You made all those pictures?"

"Yes."

"Never saw no worth in picture makin'," said the green skirted woman.

Margaret tensed.

The woman gave a smile. "Please forgive me. I didn't intend any offense. I just meant to say that I never thought abou' it much 'afore I saw that article of yours, and now that I have, I want to see more. I'm Mrs. Gunn. You must come for tea while you're here."

"Yes," said the second woman as she held out a gloved hand. "Mrs. Patterson. You must come around for tea. We'd all like to hear your stories and see more of your pictures."

The women's faces brightened as they extended the invitation. "I would be very pleased to have tea," Margaret replied.

Mrs. Gunn leaned forward. "Pardon my question, Mrs. Talbot, but why did you come in August?"

"Aye," said Mrs. Patterson. "You've missed the worst of the black flies, but it's still hotter than all blazes. You should have waited a month and come in September. That's the best time."

Margaret laughed. "Unfortunately we have a deadline to meet. Publishers don't care about the season or how uncomfortable it is."

"Well, you just come around to tea," said Mrs. Gunn. "I live in the yellow house next to the church."

Margaret promised to visit, feeling a sudden affection for the two women. They made their farewells and left the store.

Through the window, Margaret could see that John still sat alone in the wagon, his attention focused on the magazine. She reached into her pocket. MacLeod blushed deep red and turned his head. She felt herself blush as well. "Excuse me, Mr. MacLeod. I was just getting a pencil."

He turned back slowly, one eye still closed. "City folk have different ways."

"I'm sorry. I didn't mean to embarrass you. I was just going to make some quick sketches, if you'll permit me."

MacLeod nodded his head. "I don't believe I won't."

It took Margaret a moment to work out that the double negative meant MacLeod had no objection. She drew the interior of the store, the long counter made of wide spruce boards held in place with wooden dowels, the glass jars of candies, the bolts of cloth, the ploughs and saws and hammers. Finally, she drew a likeness of the clerk.

"Thank you, Mr. MacLeod."

She left the shop and decided to walk a little farther.

At an intersection she began to draw the one-room schoolhouse with its red-shingle siding and tall, white-trimmed windows. A girl in a plain dress and mobcap watched her intently before approaching. "You're the woman from away who draws for magazines."

"Yes. I'm Margaret Talbot." She extended her hand.

The girl nervously reached out with her own. "Eleanor McDonald." She curtsied. "Pleased to meet you. Mrs. MacKay said you and your husband had arrived with James Duncan and you'd drawn a picture o' Angus in the Lamont Brothers' store."

Margaret remembered the names of the two women she had met as being Gunn and Patterson, and she was certain she had not mentioned James Duncan to anyone. "Word of our arrival seems to be spreading."

"Well, not too fast. I heard from Mrs. MacKay who was hangin' wash when her sister come by and she had just talked to Liam Black who had come in from his logging camp to buy some nails which the Lamont Brothers just got a new stock in from Halifax and Liam is married to Mrs. Patterson's daughter Emily and so he stopped to pay his respects. So, you like makin' these drawings, do you?"

Margaret smiled at the whirlwind explanation. "Yes. Do you do any drawing yourself?"

"Oh, no. Mama says it's a waste o' time."

Margaret suppressed a laugh as she continued down a narrow street. She turned a corner and drew in a sharp gasp. Before her was the burned-out hulk of a brick building. The inner walls and roof were caved in. The brick was cracked and covered with soot. The air was heavy with the smell of burned wood. Men worked to shore up a wall with timbers as people stopped to stare for a moment before moving on, all the while giving the building a wide berth. In front, a charred sign read "*Glasen Hotel*".

A scratchy voice came from behind. "Are ya' proud a' ya' work, witch?"

Margaret turned to find a short, fat woman with gray streaked hair partially covered by a shawl. She wore black, lace mittens that had been designed so as to leave the fingers exposed.

Margaret said, "I'm sorry, were you addressing me?"

The old woman looked at the smoking ruins. "You've brought death and destruction to Glasen, but you'll do no more harm." She took a long knife from the folds of her dress. "I know what you are. The others are fooled but I have second sight. Your murderous ways are over."

CHAPTER TWO

Margaret held her sketch pad in front of her chest. "Are you mad?"

The woman drove the knife into the dirt street in front of her and took out a leather pouch that smelled rancid. "De'il be gone."

Margaret took a step back from the knife. This crazy woman could pull it from the ground and stab her at any time. She drew herself tall and adopted a stern look. "Stand aside."

"The curse is set. You cann'a escape, run as you may. Return to your master, whore of Satan." The old woman turned and walked away, leaving the knife stuck in the ground. Margaret stood there for a moment and stared at the knife, before pulling it out and walking back to the wagon.

James Duncan sat on the driver's bench. John had gotten down from the wagon and was speaking with a well-dressed, middle-aged man. They both looked up as she approached. John said, "Where have you been? We have a problem. The hotel has burned down."

"I know." She hurriedly relayed the story of the old woman and showed John the knife.

John reached out toward Margaret, stopped, and lowered his arms. "Are you hurt?"

"No. More confused."

John looked around. "Did you see where she went?"

The other man spoke in a voice that gave only the slightest hint of a lilt. "Mrs. Talbot, please accept my deepest apologies for this incident. I am Phillip Lamont."

Margaret said, "Do you know who did this?"

Phillip sighed. "I know very well who is responsible for this. Unfortunately, it is not the first time she has embarrassed our village."

John pointed back down the street. "Then arrest her. If she's done this before, you should have put her away already. Threatening women with knives, what kind of place is this?"

"I would feel precisely the same if I were you, Mr. Talbot, and I cannot possibly offer any kind of excuse for her actions. She's not going anywhere and will be brought to justice, I assure you. Please, do not judge us all by her actions. She is one person in a village of over a thousand, all of whom are extremely excited over your visit and honored that you would come to make an article about us."

Margaret smiled, looked at John and then back to Phillip Lamont. "Thank you, Mr. Lamont. I have, in fact, spoken with several people in Glasen. Except for this one person, everyone has made me feel quite welcome."

John started to say something, then stopped.

Phillip smiled. "Thank you, Mrs. Talbot. You are most gracious to say so in light of your experience. Please allow me to extend the hospitality of my home."

Phillip Lamont's two-story house was larger than any other in Glasen. The white clapboard siding was topped by a red tile roof. Gingerbread detail adorned the eaves with two chimneys capped by ornamental brickwork. A half-hexagonal entryway extended up to the second story. All the windows on the second floor had rounded top sashes. The house stood on a small rise overlooking the harbor.

Two boys, neither of them older than ten, stepped out of the front door. Phillip helped Margaret down from the wagon and motioned for the boys to come forward. "My sons, David and James. Boys, help take their things into the house. Set them in the entry hall." The brothers followed the instructions with intense concentration as they carried the smaller bags and hatboxes while Duncan took in the larger trunks.

John jumped to the ground. "Mr. Lamont. In all honesty I must tell you that I have grave reservations about continuing the article, given the open hostility Margaret encountered and the lack of accommodations."

Margaret listened as her husband fell into his lecture mode, giving Phillip little chance to do anything but nod his head. She cleared her throat. "I realize these matters are of the utmost importance, but just at this moment, I would dearly love to freshen up."

Phillip showed relief at the interruption as he put his hand to his forehead. "Oh, Mrs. Talbot, please forgive me. I don't know where my manners went off to. You see, I've been a widower for some time and there's naught but me and the boys. I've quite forgotten the needs of a beautiful woman."

The compliment felt wonderfully pleasant and she smiled. "You are quite forgiven, sir."

Phillip called into the house. "David, run down and ask your Aunt and Uncle up for tea at half past."

"Yes, Papa."

The young boy ran down the road. Margaret looked after him. "He's quite a little man."

"Yes, he is, though he misses his mother sorely. We all do."

"I'm sorry."

"Thank you. She was a good woman who led a fine life. Now she's safe in the arms of our Lord, where we'll meet again someday." He crossed himself and smiled, though there was wetness in his eyes.

Margaret cocked her head at John. "So, we're staying?"

"What kind of a question is that?"

She spread her hands. "There might be more spooky old women in Glasen."

"Save your sarcasm for the editors." He paid James Duncan and instructed him to return in eight weeks, while Margaret followed Phillip into the parlor. A fireplace occupied the middle of one wall. In front of it, a small sofa created a quiet, intimate place to sit and watch the flames. The fireplace was clearly more for show than warmth, as a small coal-burning stove stood in one corner.

The rest of the room held a second, larger sofa and four chairs. Around the room were tables covered with books, boxes, decanters, and oil lamps.

A portrait of Queen Victoria sat by itself on a small table with a black ribbon draped over the frame. It had been seven months since the passing of the eighty-one year old monarch, yet Margaret had seen the deep love Canadians still held for the queen and their continued outpouring of grief.

An oddly-shaped clock stood against one of the walls. It was a good six feet tall. At the top, the dark oak case was about eight inches across, just wide enough to contain the face. As the case extended down, it curved out on either side to about twelve inches before tapering back at the base.

Phillip said, "It's a bow clock, designed to use the least amount of wood possible. At the top, where the pendulum is anchored, there's less need for clearance, so it's built slim. In the middle, it's wide to accommodate the swing of the pendulum. The base tapers in again with just enough width to keep it from tipping over."

Margaret ran her hand over the curved shape. "Ingenious. Who thought of it?"

"I couldn't say. A schooner captain brought it from Scotland. I've seen several others abou'." Though Phillip's speech was generally flat, he, like everyone else, still clipped some words.

She sat on the sofa. John chose a chair on the opposite side of the room.

James's excited voice echoed in the entryway. "Uncle Alistair. Auntie Anna." Phillip's brother and sister-in-law walked into the living room with the two boys following close behind.

Anna was thin with brilliant white hair. Her dress, a flowery pink and yellow print, was a few years out of fashion.

Alistair was fat and balding with gray sideburns that drooped down across thick jowls. He wore a plaid waistcoat of which the two bottom buttons were undone. Across his hefty middle was a gold watch chain that he fingered as he sat.

Anna placed a small, cloth-covered basket on a table. Phillip retrieved a tea tray from a sideboard and looked to his two sons. "Now you boys get out from underfoot." The brothers whined and protested, but in the end they left to play outside.

Anna took the tea tray from Phillip, placed some scones and butter on it from the basket, and served. "Never trust a man to know what to do when guests arrive," she said to Margaret, but with a wink to the men.

Margaret took a bite of a scone, closed her eyes and gave a satisfied sigh. "These are wonderful, Anna. I always thought scones were hard and crumbly."

"Oh, these are fresh, dear. They'll be stale when they've set around for a day."

Margaret finished another bite. "I don't think there's much chance of that happening."

John said, "Mr. Lamont, I imagine that, as the local magistrate, you see some interesting things."

Phillip shook his head. "Not really, Mr. Talbot. The local gossip in the shops is a better source for your article. Most of the cases are for drunkenness or disturbing the peace."

"I see. How long have you been the magistrate?"

"Six years now, though it's not a full time job. My day is largely spent at the dry goods store."

"Have the Lamonts always lived in Glasen?"

Alistair fingered his watch fob and pursed his lips. Margaret realized this would not be a quick answer. As soon as they'd arrived in Nova Scotia, she had found a rich storytelling tradition in every home, shop, and inn. They were stories from the lives of the people, the everyday incidents which, when presented with great theater, were anything but ordinary.

After a dramatic pause, Alistair leaned forward. "The three of us were born on Caribou Island to the west, in the Northumberland Strait. My grandfather came over from Scotland a century ago and settled on the island with a couple of other families. Anna was born a MacKay. Her folk came across on the ship Hector, with the first permanent Scottish immigrants in 1773."

He went on to tell of how he married Anna and fished the waters around the Northumberland Strait. It was a hard life with little reward. Then, he heard about the gold strike on the eastern shore of Nova Scotia in 1862.

Anna said, "We traveled to Halifax by coach. There we were: Alistair, the two girls, and me. We paid two dollars each for passage to Glasen by schooner. It was abou' all the money we had, and my mother said we would come to ruin for our greed and folly."

Alistair told how he went out prospecting every day and how hard the work was, especially in winter. He managed to dig out some ore, but it was barely enough. The more gold that came in, the higher the prices rose for everything. There were too many men, and companies were forming from as far away as Toronto and the states to stake out large claims.

He stopped to take a sip of tea. "Our money was running low and it had been a week since I had dug up anything. I told Anna we had best go back to Caribou Island while we still had enough for passage and some fishing gear."

He turned to Anna. "Then you gave a sigh, and I'll never forget this. You said, 'I guess that's all we can do. With the prices rising like they are, the only ones gettin' rich are the merchants.' I stopped and looked at her, and the idea just fell into place. The next day I took what money and gold we had left, booked passage to Halifax, bought as many pants, shirts, shovels, and picks as I could, came back to Glasen, and set up shop. Three years later I sent word for Phillip to join us. He wasn't much older than David, but he worked with me in the shop every day and with our hands, we built most of this village."

John said, "That's a wonderful story. Exactly the kind of thing our editor wants."

Margaret said, "We should probably send word to George and let him know we arrived."

"Quite right. Is there a telegraph office in the village?"

Phillip said, "There's no telegraph, but we do have a telephone exchange that can reach Halifax. I have a telephone here in the house and there's one in the store that we use for placing orders. I'm certain one of our suppliers in Halifax would be happy to send a cable to New York for you."

"How odd to have a telephone line but no telegraph."

"It just worked out that way. No one seemed to have a need for a telegraph at first and then the exchange went in some twenty years ago, largely through the influence of Alexander Bell building his home in Baddeck. Quite a few villages and towns put them in. I think we have three dozen or so telephones in Glasen."

"And that's abou' three dozen more than are required," said Alistair. "No one needs to talk to anyone that quickly, except for a doctor."

"And who would the doctor speak to if no one else had a telephone?"

Anna said, "Now you two stop that with company and all." She looked to Margaret. "I declare, sometimes they're worse than the boys—if there's actually any difference."

Phillip's face reddened. He cleared his throat and said, "Mrs. Talbot. Would you please repeat the story of what happened just before we met?"

Margaret relayed the events of the old woman.

Anna nodded her head. "That can only be Beth Ramsey."

Phillip poured milk into his cup and added some fresh tea. "She's not a truly evil person, but she often does the devil's work in the name of the Lord, so to speak."

Margaret said, "What caused the fire at the hotel?"

"I'd say the boiler went," said Phillip.

Alistair set his cup down. "Broke windows for a block around. When we clear the rubble out of the basement we plan to have Will Gunn take a look. He used to be a locomotive fireman. He's seen many a blown boiler."

"Why did she accuse me of burning down the hotel with magic?" Margaret asked.

Anna said, "Most of us in Glasen came from Scotland, or our forebears did, and we all remember the Celtic tales of fairies and sprites. They're the kind of stories you tell the wee bairn. Everyone in Glasen goes to mass on Sunday. We all know what's real and what isn't, except for Beth Ramsey. To her, the stories are more than legends, they're as real as flesh and blood, and she's muddled it all together with the teachings of the church. I don't know what's wrong with her, or why she fears anyone from away so much. When she heard you were coming she was livid and warned us that the devil rode with you."

"Well, she's harmless enough," said Alistair. "Now, as to the hotel being unavailable, we had to decide where you could stay. Most folk were willing to take you in, but few had any place to put you. Families run large here and every bed counts. We would take you in, however, unlike my brother, who enjoys the trappings of extravagance, Anna and I live in a modest house which suits our needs but leaves no room for overnight guests."

Phillip glared at his brother, and then said, "You can sleep under my roof tonight, but you cannot stay any longer. It wouldn't do for me, a widower, to be alone in the house with a married woman."

John gave a short laugh. "Margaret and I both have men and women visit us in New York when one or the other of us is out. It's just a part of life."

"Well, this is not New York, and it's not a part of our lives. I dare not place myself in a compromising position. The two of you leave in eight weeks. I must continue to live here."

Alistair folded his hands over his belly. "Don't worry, Mr. Talbot. We've taken to makin' all the arrangements. You'll be staying with Ian and Sara Grant just outside the village. It's not an overly large house, but they have no children and there should be room for you to work. Your wife can help out abou' the house to keep herself busy."

Margaret wasn't certain which angered her more—Alistair's

insinuation that she had nothing better to do than keep house, or the fact that he referred to her in the third person, as if she weren't there.

She said, "I am gratified by your concern that I might become bored and listless outside the ten or fifteen hours a day I will spend illustrating our article. Perhaps John can join me in washing clothes or sweeping up in between the time he will be conducting interviews and writing. We are, after all, partners, taking on the same responsibility and earning the same honors."

The room fell silent. Peter looked up at the ceiling. Alistair blushed deep red. John looked at Margaret with a scowl.

Anna collected the cups as though nothing had been said. "Well, magazine articles can wait until tomorrow. We're having Father Williams over to supper and there's plenty to be done." She ended with a gaze at Margaret.

Perhaps the words had come because she was tired. Perhaps they tumbled out because of the threat of Beth Ramsey. Perhaps those things had just compounded with all the times arrogant men had tried to thwart her. No matter the reason, the last thing she wanted to do was make enemies of their only friends in Glasen. She regretted her outburst, but did not apologize for it. "Is there anything I can do to help, Anna?"

"Why, how kind of you to offer. If you'll bring the tea things along, we'll start the mutton."

John said, "Actually, Margaret and I do work as a team. It would be better if she stayed to discuss business."

The brothers stared at him. Alistair fingered his watch fob yet again. Anna waited silently. Margaret picked up the teapot. "I really would prefer to help Anna in the kitchen, if you don't mind. I'm sure she can tell me quite a bit about Glasen."

In a world where she had few legal rights merely because of her gender, and could not even vote to elect representatives to grant those rights, John had always encouraged and supported her to fight for equal recognition. Before the stillbirth, he had actively worked with her for woman's suffrage. He walked with Margaret in marches and endured taunts from other men standing on the sidelines who shouted, "Go back to the kitchen" and "Don't worry your pretty little heads." John lost his membership in a prominent club over the march, yet continued to work with Margaret.

She had admired him for his courage and his undaunted defense of her ability to work in publishing. Yet, no matter how many times she tried to tell him, he was oblivious to the fact that she was trained as a painter and had never really wanted to work in publishing to begin with.

She followed Anna past the stairs in the entry hall, where their trunks stood next to another coal stove. They walked through the dining room and into the kitchen. The room contained a table and chairs, a sink with a pump but no stove, and only a pipe extending from a narrow, brick chimney.

Margaret looked around. "Is this the kitchen?"

Anna, who had continued walking toward another door, stopped and turned. "Only in the cold weather, dear. This is the winter kitchen. Far too hot to cook in here this time of year. The stove's been moved to the summer kitchen out back. Keeps the rest of the house from heating up."

Margaret followed Anna through the other door to find a complete second kitchen with a pantry, two tables, chairs, a deep sink, hand pump, and, this time, a wood-burning stove. The walls were bare lumber painted white. Green trim outlined two large open windows set on walls opposite to each other. On the wall between them was a door leading outside.

The stove was lit, presumably by one of the boys, and Margaret understood immediately why it was moved as far away from the rest of the house as possible during the humid summer.

Anna took off her hat, removed her coat and hung them on hooks next to the door. "You get down to your blouse too, dear. Visiting's over." Margaret gratefully removed her hat and jacket and hung them next to Anna's.

David and James, oblivious to the temperature, ran in and out in some sort of catch me game. Anna broke a scone in two, spread some jam on the pieces, and offered them to the boys. They giggled, took the booty, and sat at the smaller table to eat.

The two women washed the dishes and set them back in the cupboard. Margaret picked up the teapot. "This is a very large house for Phillip to take care of by himself, especially with the boys. Couldn't he hire servants?"

"Alistair has suggested it many times, especially after..." Anna stopped, looked toward the boys, and then whispered into Margaret's ear, "After poor Lucille died of the smallpox. He keeps saying he will, but hasn't yet."

Anna set a pot under the spigot of an indoor pump and worked the handle. When the pot was filled she placed it on the stove where it hissed and steamed as the water on the outside boiled off. "You'll like the Grants. Sara is very nice."

"She's a seal," said David with his mouth full.

Margaret turned and looked at him. "I beg your pardon?"

"A seal," said James.

Anna came over and wiped their faces with a damp cloth. "Oh, nonsense."

"She talks to the seals. I've seen her."

"She dances with them at midnight," said David.

"Don't say such things." Anna crossed herself. "You've never been out at midnight, and the devil would have you if you were."

"Can we have more scones, Auntie?"

"You little scamps!" The boys giggled. "Well, all right, but take them outside, and don't tell your father I'm ruinin' your supper." They took one scone each and ran out the door.

Anna shook her head. "I spoil those boys too much. They remind me of my girls when they were young. Do you have any children, dear?"

In the two years since the stillbirth, Margaret had been told by doctors, nurses, clergy and friends to forget what had happened. It was for the best, they told her. Dwelling on matters would only prolong her recovery.

At first, she'd been too ill from nearly dying to muster the strength for an argument. When she'd recovered enough, she asked if the baby was a boy or a girl, where the baby had been buried, why the baby had died. Everyone ignored her questions, especially John, who would leave the house without a word when she persisted. A sense of dread grew inside her. Sometimes she doubled over in pain from cramps in her abdomen. Medical examinations could find no physical cause.

She'd begun to have thoughts of dying to be with her baby or to punish herself for causing the child's death, but mostly, it seemed her only escape from the overwhelming sadness.

In desperation, she'd forced the memory to the back of her mind. After a while, it seemed to help. She began to eat regularly and was able to leave the house. Soon after, she started back to work. It felt as if she had recovered completely. Still, there were nights when she woke with panic-stricken nightmares.

Standing there in Phillip Lamont's kitchen, working on an assignment, she expected herself to have a detached, unemotional reaction to Anna's question. Instead, she felt the old cramping pain press up from her gut.

This is ridiculous. Get a hold of yourself. Her throat tightened as her eyes burned. She fought to concentrate on something else, anything else.

Margaret turned her face toward the drain board. "We don't have any children yet."

"I guess it would be difficult, with all your traveling."

"Yes." She swallowed hard, forced a smile, and put away the last cup. "What did the boys mean about seals?"

"Oh, just idle gossip."

"Don't people like Mrs. Grant?"

"We all like her, dear. Very much. Sara is the sweetest person you could ever want to know. And she's very good to Ian. He came to Glasen almost twenty years ago. The only thing he'd say abou' his past was that his first wife, Lizzie, and their son, Samuel, had died at sea. He took to fishing the waters in a dory, went to mass each Sunday and to every ceilidh."

The word sounded to her ear like *kay-lee*, with the emphasis on *kay*. "I'm sorry. What was that?"

"Ceilidh? It means 'a visit' in the old Gaelic, but it's come to be used for dances or gatherings where neighbors meet and young folks court. Widows and widowers court, too, but not Ian.

"Most men remarry pretty quick around here. It's just too hard raising a family and making a living. Phillip is overdue, but he has his eye on Mary Ross, and she's cast back an eye or two herself. Ian stayed a widower. Whoever Lizzie was, she had a powerful hold on him."

As she spoke, Anna slid a leg of lamb into the oven and stoked the fire.

"One day, Ian went out fishin' and didn't return that night. After a few days, we thought he had drowned. It's a dangerous life on the sea. Then, he came back with Sara in the boat as if nothing unusual had happened. I remember how she stood on the dock, her eyes wide as she trembled slightly. She spoke just two words, 'Hello', and 'Yes', though she pronounced it *Yesh*. Whenever Sara went abou', Ian was with her. He invited few guests into his house. Alistair is Ian's closest friend, so we were an exception.

"In the first few weeks of her arrival it was clear that things you and I take for granted, like cooking or having tea or wearing clothes, were a mystery to Sara. I went over one day when Ian was out fishing and found her with a corset on top of her dress." Anna pointed to her head. "Alistair and I were afraid she might be impaired."

"One day, she suddenly understood everything. She knew exactly how to act at mass, was perfectly mannered at tea, knew when to laugh and when to frown and when to nod her head. Still, everything she did was a little unusual, almost too precise, like someone who learned cooking from a book without ever having tasted food. It wasn't much of a leap for those like Beth Ramsey to think she had magical powers and the rumors started that she was a selkie."

Margaret sat down at the larger table. "I've heard that word in Ireland. They're some kind of magical sprites, aren't they?"

"A fairy folk. Old myths say they live in the ocean as seals and help sailors or fishermen in distress. On the Eve of St. John, the selkies are supposed to swim to shore, remove their seal skins, and, in the form of men and women, dance in the moonlight."

"So that's what James meant."

"Children learn the legends early. Some say that selkie maidens can take human husbands. There are stories were selkies can take human or seal form at will and other tales where selkies can take on human form only once to leave the sea, and if they touch the water again, they return to their seal forms forever."

"What a remarkable story," said Margaret.

"There are many such tales brought over from Scotland," said Anna. "But they're just fluff and nonsense. Most folk here and abou' know that people don't turn into seals or witches or anything else, no matter what Beth Ramsey may say."

A knock came at the rear door. Anna opened it and a middle-aged woman stepped inside. Her dark brown hair was fixed in a tight bun. The woman nodded her head. "Evening, Anna. I was just passing by and thought I'd come in for a moment. Oh. I see you have a visitor."

Anna stared back at the woman. "Flora. This is Phillip's house. *I'm* a visitor."

"Well, aren't you going to introduce me?"

Anna shook her head in resignation. "Margaret Talbot, may I introduce my cousin, Flora Brown."

Flora took Margaret's hand. "Not Margaret Talbot, the illustrator?"

Margaret kept a neutral expression. "Yes."

"I am so thrilled to meet you. I had no idea you were coming to Glasen. You're such an inspiration. I've always loved art and pictures. It brings me such joy. You know, my son, Thomas, is very talented with a pencil."

Margaret raised an eyebrow. "Oh, is he?"

"Yes, I asked him to wait outside. I was only going to step in for a moment. Would you mind terribly if he came in to meet you? It would mean a great deal to him."

Anna waged a finger at her cousin. "Now Flora, don't you go embarrassing the village like this."

Margaret laughed. Both women stopped and stared at her, Flora with an indignant look on her face. Margaret put a hand to her mouth.

"I'm sorry. Please, don't be angry. It's just that the two of you are so charming, so... yourselves"

Flora's eyes widened. "And who else would we be?"

Margaret composed herself. "Mrs. Brown, I am constantly asked to see the works of this budding artist or that, and I have a complete stock of answers to avoid having to tell doting parents that the apple of their eye has no talent whatsoever. But, I'll make a bargain with you. Bring Thomas in and I'll look at his work, which I am certain he just happens to have with him. But I will tell him the truth about it, good or bad. Is that acceptable?"

After a pause, Flora agreed.

Thomas came in. Tall and thin, the twenty year old wore a white shirt with no collar and dungarees held up by suspenders. He removed a bowler hat and twisted it around in a circle with callused hands. "I apologize for my mother's behavior, Mrs. Talbot. It is truly an honor to meet you."

"No apologies are necessary, Thomas. Here, let's sit at the big table. Show me what you have."

He opened some oil skin wrappings and took out three pieces of paper. Margaret let her eyes scan across the drawings, flickering quickly from one to the other, never settling for more than a few seconds. It was a technique that gave her an overall impression and let the important aspects catch her eye.

These pictures refused such summary inspection. Each drew her attention. Each demanded she look at it. The first was a fishing dory pulled up on the beach for repair. She imagined running her hands over it and feeling splinters. It was a tired boat, used and exhausted. The flaking paint, the loose boards, the weathered oars, all imbued the scene with a sense of sadness that spoke of far more than a simple boat.

The second picture was a gull in flight. The bird floated easily on the breeze, its eyes scanning the ground for food. Each feather was perfect, the head cocked just right.

It was the third drawing that spoke clearest to her. A man past middle age wrapped his arm around the waist of a young woman. The man's beard was flecked with white. The woman had turned her head to look up at him. Her eyes were large and dark. She grinned with youth, hopeful and happy. He smiled back, though his face held a hint of sadness.

Margaret picked up the portrait and stepped closer to the window for more light. "Thomas, this is magnificent. You have captured far more than a likeness of these people. This is a moment in their lives, held forever on paper." She paused and studied the young woman's face. "That's Sara Grant, isn't it?"

"Yes, ma'am."

"So, this must be Ian." Margaret continued to study the picture. "When did you draw this?"

"Last month. It was Sunday morning. They were abou' to go into mass when all of a sudden he grabs her round the waist like that and she turns and gives him that smile. I was right behind them and saw it all. After Mass I did some chores, sat down under a tree, and made the picture."

"Do you mean you saw this for just an instant and kept that image in your head for hours before sketching it out?"

"Yes ma'am. I do all my drawing under that tree."

"This is remarkable. Do you do any paintings?"

"Oh no, ma'am. I just draw with a pencil."

Margaret looked to Anna, "Do you think there's enough for them to stay for dinner?" She turned back to Thomas. "I really want to talk about your drawings. I know some people who should see them. How often does your mail go out?"

As she spoke, Thomas smiled. Then, he grinned broadly.

Flora watched her son intently. "You've had a long trip, Mrs. Talbot. We can talk more tomorrow."

Margaret waved her hand in the air. "Thank you, but I'm not tired. Thomas, can you do some more sketches for me tonight?"

"Well, I don't know. I do all my drawing under the tree." His eyes became glassy as his arms started to shake. "Do you really think they're good?"

Anna said, "Flora's right. We should talk tomorrow."

Margaret started to repeat that she wasn't tired when Thomas's eyes rolled up into his lids. A strangling rasp came from his throat and he fell to the floor, his body convulsed, his fingers clenched and his feet kicked blindly.

Flora fell to her knees beside her son. "It's all right, my Tommy. Mother is here. You're safe, my baby."

Thomas continued to shake in violent seizures. Margaret looked to Flora and then to Anna.

Anna shook her head. "When the boy was three, he was in a field of sheep. Some city fools up hunting got bored. They were dead drunk and came staggering over to the edge of the herd and started firing.

"As docile as sheep are, a frightened herd will run over anything, and a wee bairn isn't much to stop them. He near died. Ever since, the palsy comes to him without warning. It's worse when he gets excited. The doctor calls it 'epa' something."

"Epilepsy," said Flora coldly. "Your praise overwhelmed him. I should have seen it."

Margaret was not a cruel person. Her compassion in drives for the poor was well known. But years of traveling the world and illustrating articles on famine, flood, war, fire, and pestilence had left her slightly distanced from the suffering of those she and John reported on. She was surprised when her eyes suddenly teared over.

Anna took Margaret's hand. "It's not your fault, dear."

The men ran into the kitchen. Phillip said, "I'll get Doctor Ferguson."

"No," said Flora. "He's comin' 'round. All of you clear off now. You know how embarrassed he gets."

Thomas gave a jerk, got to his hands and knees, and looked around. "What are you staring at?" He stood shakily and eyed the assemblage one by one. When he looked at Margaret, he bit his lower lip and ran out the back door. Flora collected her son's pictures and followed.

CHAPTER THREE

Father Williams was a soft-spoken man in his late fifties with a Bostonian accent that held the vowels long, dropped the letter '*R*' at the end of some words and added it into the middle of others.

Margaret glanced out the window of the dining room. A cloudburst earlier had cleared the humid air and left behind a slightly cool evening. She cut a thin slice of lamb. "I hope I can persuade you to sit for a portrait, Father."

Williams smiled. "I would be honored, madam. Now, how did the two of you meet and start writing these articles? That's what I want to know."

John picked up the stemware in front of him and absently twirled it between his thumb and forefinger. "I was working for the *New York Evening Post* when the blizzard of eighty-eight dropped almost two feet of snow on the city with thirty foot drifts. The winds were blowing at seventy-five miles an hour and it was very difficult to get around. It occurred to me that some illustrations would increase the impact of the story.

"I had a friend who worked for the *Tribune*. I called him and asked if he could recommend someone. He said he was sending over M. Cooper and was certain I would be satisfied. An hour later a rather pretty young woman arrived. At first, I took her for a messenger. She very quickly set me right on that. 'I am Margaret Cooper, your illustrator,' she said, 'and nothing else. Is that understood?'"

John cleared his throat and took a sip of water.

"I'd worked with many illustrators. Most produced crude caricatures. Not Margaret. The lines, the shadows, the details of her pictures were far more than just illustrations. They were a window into the reality of what she drew, almost as if you could step through the paper and touch it.

"The article was a fantastic success. For the first time in my career, a newspaper in another city wanted to reprint my work. I knew Margaret's illustrations were part of the reason. Other men may have felt belittled to owe their success to a woman. I knew the makings of a team, though I liked the sound of 'Talbot and Cooper' better than 'Cooper and Talbot.'

"Miss Cooper illustrated my next story and the response was even greater. Publishers loved the combination of words and pictures. We continued to work together as Talbot and Cooper until Miss Cooper consented to become Mrs. Talbot." John raised his glass to Margaret.

Everyone clapped. Margaret felt wetness in the corners of her eyes as she looked to John. Alistair stood and lifted his glass. "A toast to John and Margaret Talbot. May their lives be long and happy."

The dinner guests left. Anna made Margaret promise to call on her later in the week. John was given a spare room upstairs with a narrow bed, and Margaret was on the first floor in the sick room that was set aside for travelers or those too ill to climb stairs.

The boys had been put to bed hours before. The evening air turned suddenly cold and Phillip lit a fire. "This chill is rather unseasonable. I'll go bring some more wood in."

When Phillip left the room, Margaret stood near the fire and rubbed her hands together. "That was very nice, what you said at dinner."

John examined a wedding photograph of Phillip and Lucille. "It was all true."

"That's not what I meant. Why are we only polite to each other when other people are around?"

He rubbed his eyes. "It's too late to discuss this tonight."

"It's always too late, John. I'm afraid one day it really will be."

He stared into the flames. "Margaret, please. We've had a pleasant evening. Can't we just leave it at that?"

She turned and faced him. "But what about tomorrow evening? And the evening after?"

Margaret heard footsteps from the entry hall and quickly sat on the sofa facing the fireplace. Phillip walked in with an armful of wood. He sat it next to the hearth and stoked the flames. "Odd weather indeed, but at least a fire makes for a cozy first evening in Glasen. Lucille and I used to sit here for hours. You can just let the fire burn itself out. We'll start early tomorrow. Good night." He walked up the stairs.

John leaned against the mantle and kicked some stray ashes back into the firebox. Margaret sat in one corner of the sofa with her arms crossed tightly over her chest. He let out a sigh and sat on the sofa. "All right," he said. "Let's talk."

Margaret fidgeted with her dress as the fire crackled and smoked. The side of her body facing the flames felt warm while the other was cool. "Well," she said. "What shall we talk about?"

"You're the one who wanted to talk. You tell me."

"Can't you ever bring up a subject?"

"I don't understand what we are arguing about."

"We're not arguing. I'm just asking you what you want to talk about."

"But you brought up the subject of talking. What did you want to say?"

"Maybe I didn't want to say anything. Maybe I wanted to hear you say something."

"What?"

"I don't know."

"Then who does?"

The fire hissed. John stood up. "If we are not going to talk, I, for one, would like to get some sleep."

"No, wait. Please. It's just that what you said tonight at dinner, about how important my drawings are, was the nicest thing I've heard you say about me in a very long time. I just wish you could say things like that when no one else is around."

He sat back down. "So, you'd like me to compliment you?"

"Not like that. It would be nice if you said those things, and meant them."

"I wouldn't have said what I did if I didn't mean it."

"I'm talking about from inside, where you don't have to have someone prod you."

"Do you think I was making it up, Margaret?"

"No."

"I meant what I said tonight."

"I'm not doubting you, John. I just want you to…" She closed her eyes and dropped her chin to her chest. "You used to say nice things just to say them. Now you hardly talk to me, and it's always business." She tried to stop the tears, but they fell down her face and onto her blouse. "You used to touch me, and you don't touch me anymore. It was very nice tonight, and I just remembered how it used to be."

He sat up stiffly. "And it's not nice anymore, is that what you're saying?"

"John, what's happened to us?"

"Nothing's ever good enough for you, Margaret. There's always something you don't have."

"For God's sake, listen to me."

He gave an exasperated sigh. "Why do you think we do the articles? I try to provide for you, but you thwart me at every turn. I write and I write and I only ask you to provide the illustrations. But all you can talk about is what you think you don't have."

Her cheeks flushed. "That's all I am to you now, a drawing machine. Do you love me anymore? Did you ever?"

"What am I supposed to do? Write the articles and draw the

illustrations? Is that what you want?"

A log fell in the firebox and a blast of heat rushed into the room. Margaret's voice was calm, nearly silent. "Leave me alone."

John stood up abruptly. "Very well. I'm going to sleep. We start early. Be ready." He walked up the stairs.

Unattended, the fire soon died into cool embers. Margaret sat silently in the dark for a few minutes before standing and walking to her room. Securing the door behind her, she opened one of her steamer trunks to reveal blouses and jackets hung from a bar running from front to back.

She reached behind the clothes and pulled out a flat twenty-by-thirty inch object covered in fabric. Beneath the cloth were two artist's canvases fastened together, face to face, by specially designed tacks with two pinpoints extending from either side of brass heads. The heads formed a narrow gap that kept the canvases from touching so that any wet paint would not smear.

One canvas was blank. Margaret set that aside. The other was the partially completed portrait of a seventy-four-year-old black woman named Blossom. They had met when she and John traveled to Alabama the previous fall for an article on sharecroppers.

Margaret took a collapsible easel from the trunk and set the painting on it. She stepped back and studied it, reacquainting herself with the work. The former slave sat at a table as she stared out a window. Light washed one side of her face, throwing the other side into shadow. Her cheek rested against her left palm as her right arm lay draped across the table.

Margaret's training was a unique mixture of the conservative teachings of the Paris academies and the daring vibrancy of the Impressionists as brought back from France by American painters such as Robert Henri, one of the founders of an art movement known as *The Ashcan School*. They chose colors for emotional impact, taking painting out of the controlled studio and into the place where the subject was, be that a home or an alley.

The ideal would have been to stay with Blossom and complete the portrait from the live model. That was impossible. John had been with her every day, badgering her about the sketches, reminding her of their deadline, forbidding her to paint.

Swearing Blossom to secrecy, Margaret had begun the oil painting while John was away at the county court house. When John returned, she hid the canvas and made extensive studies in charcoal, drawings referred to by artists as cartoons, and painted at night while John slept in another room.

The sketches were now spread across her bed in Phillip Lamont's sick room. Each time she looked at the drawings, Blossom's eyes captured her. She traced her finger around their outline on the paper. "Oh, Blossom. What have you seen in seven decades?"

From the same trunk she took a palette board, some tubes of oil paint, a jar of turpentine, and four hog bristle brushes of varying sizes. After opening a window for ventilation, she mixed some paint to form light ebony. Holding one of the brushes like a fencing foil, she extended her reach fully and began to work on Blossom's arms.

As Margaret painted she stepped back for perspective, moved forward to paint some more, then stepped back again. This dance continued while she worked.

She imagined Blossom as a slave, picking cotton with those long, thin arms. In her mind sweat trickled Blossom's back as she stooped in the fields from dawn to dusk.

One of Robert Henri's art lectures came to mind.

> *"Don't worry about imitating nature. You're expressing an idea. Always keep that in the back of your mind until it is expressed on the canvas, no matter how long it takes; days, weeks, or years. Time doesn't matter. The work is complete when that special thing is said."*

That special thing continued to elude Margaret. She knew it had to do with the strength Blossom had endured through slavery, two children dead from illness, another sold at auction, and a husband beaten to death.

Margaret brushed on paint, stood back, scraped paint off with a flat knife, adjusted the color and brushed on some more. The arms remained flat and lifeless. In the sketches they were tempered by years of struggle. The oil showed none of this. The more Margaret tried to correct it, the more frustrated she became. The oil would not obey her as the pencil did. She sat down on the bed and put her head in her hands. "Blossom, what are you trying to tell me? If I had half the strength of your arms I'd know what to do."

She felt a tickle on the back of her neck, looked up and took in a sharp breath. Someone was looking at her through the window. Then she realized it wasn't *someone*, it was some*thing*. A seal stared unblinkingly at her. Margaret got to her feet and the seal dropped out of sight. She leaned outside. There was a wooden box just beneath the window, but no sign of the seal. It could not have moved that fast across the ground on flippers. Perhaps she had imagined it. She looked down. There was the wet outline of flippers on the otherwise dry box.

Quarter past five in the morning came very early for Margaret.

"If you expect to talk to a fisherman," said Phillip through the closed door, "you'd best get used to this hour."

She chose a white dress fashioned in the lingerie style with layers of chiffon and lace for her first meeting with the Grants. Instead of donning high button shoes, which were the fashion, she wore men's boots with flat soles that were concealed beneath the hem of her dress. They gave her support and stability that shoes designed for woman and fashion did not.

John sat at the large table in the summer kitchen with the boys. Phillip stood at the stove cooking a stack of pancakes. "Ah, good morning to you, Mrs. Talbot. Would you be having any pancakes, or would you like porridge, or both? We have maple syrup and some butter in the crock."

"Thank you. Those pancakes look very good. I don't think we've had any since that story about the logging camp, have we, John?"

He looked out the window. "I'm sure we haven't."

Phillip flipped pancakes on the griddle. "You've made an excellent choice. James, come take this plate to the table. Please, sit down, Mrs.

Talbot. You'll find us a little less formal here than in New York."

Three knocks came on the door and Anna Lamont stepped through. "I was just saying to Alistair last night that I haven't been out to see Sara and Ian for a while, so he suggested that it might be nice for me to drive you out there this morning and let poor Phillip get on with his business."

Phillip continued flipping pancakes. "That would be nice of you, Anna." He turned quickly to Margaret and John. "Not to say that I dislike your company, Mr. and Mrs. Talbot."

Margaret laughed. John gave a tepid smile.

After breakfast, Phillip helped John load the trunks into the surrey. It was black with a leather awning and two padded benches.

The largest trunk containing Margaret's hidden painting wouldn't fit. Phillip promised to deliver them later in the day. Anxiety grew at the thought of someone opening the trunk to discover the painting, but she said nothing lest she draw attention to the trunk.

In the pre-dawn glow, Margaret got out her sketchbook and peered hard into the growing light. From houses along every road, men emerged wearing high boots, long rubber coats, and bowl-shaped, waterproof hats called sou'westers, whose brims tapered back over their necks. Each walked toward the water.

Regardless of a home's size, the windows in each shone with the flickerless light of oil lamps. The pinpoints spread across the valley and up the hillside. It seemed to Margaret that the stars had descended from the sky to the valley floor.

Wives, lamps in hand, stepped into the streets with their husbands and kissed them goodbye. From inside the houses, the faces of children pressed against windows. Wives and children waved as each husband-father-fisherman walked away into the damp air.

The harbor came into view. It reminded her of the fishing boat Thomas had drawn. "Anna, I'd really like to speak with Thomas Brown again. The boy has talent that should not go to waste."

"Aye, that's true enough, but I don't think he'll want to be seein' you. You've witnessed one of his fits, and he barely tolerates us knowing abou' them. He won't come to you again, even though you hold everything he's ever wanted."

At the wharf, most of the fishermen climbed into dories—small, oared boats with flat bottoms and high sides. Moored to the wharf, next to a brick warehouse, was a schooner with two tall masts. On her deck were eight dories arranged in two stacks. One man coiled rope at the bow while another sat at the stern smoking a pipe.

Margaret pointed across the water. "What's wrong with that ship? It doesn't seem to be leaving with the rest."

Anna smiled. "You'll want to get the terms right for your article. Boats are 'she', not 'it.' And they don't leave, they 'put out.' You're looking at the *Scarlet Lion*. Hugh Drummond, there with the pipe, is her master. The dory men putting out now are inland fishermen and can row in and out as they please. They'll let out their hook lines close into the coast and trawl till they catch their fill. Then they'll row back here, unload, and go out for a second or third catch. *The Lion* has to wait for the tide before she can sail, and that's a good hour from now. Hugh will take her out beyond the shallow bank for ten or twelve days, where the dory men will trawl in deep water and fill the hull of the schooner."

"Does Ian Grant ever fish with Drummond?"

Anna kept the horse moving. "Ian fishes alone."

They followed the road southwest, retracing the way she and John had come the day before. It skirted the shore around twisting bends. The light brightened, and on the horizon the spark of the rising sun flashed into brilliant radiance. Margaret shielded her eyes. Within seconds the full disk climbed into the sky, giving color and shape to the landscape.

Smoke rose from the chimney of the Grants' house. Anna turned the horse toward the front door. It was just as Margaret remembered it from the day before; white clapboards, green trim, no porch, ladder hanging down the steep pitch of the roof next to the stone chimney. Drawn curtains cut off any view of the interior.

A bearded man stood at the threshold with the door barely open. A young woman peeked out from behind him. Margaret immediately recognized them as Ian and Sara Grant.

One of Ian's hands was wrapped around a pipe that protruded from his mouth, the other firmly placed in his pocket.

Anna pulled the horse to a stop. "Good morning, Ian, Sara."

Ian nodded his head stiffly. "Morning, Anna."

"These are the Talbots, John and Margaret."

John got out and extended his hand as he walked to the door. "Mr. Grant. Mrs. Grant. My wife and I are very grateful for your hospitality. I assure you, we will disturb your normal life as little as possible."

Ian took the pipe from his mouth and jabbed the stem toward John's chest. "Let me be completely clear, Mr. Talbot. You and your wife are here because Phillip and Alistair want you to write this article. I will not stand against their wishes. But I will not have you sticking your nose in my business. And leave Sara alone. She has plenty to do and no time for foolishness." Though he had a slight lilt from the local dialect, his voice was distinctly American.

"Ian!" Anna got down off the surrey. "This has all been sorted out and I see no reason to insult our guests."

Ian chewed hard the stem of his pipe. "There are things a man doesn't want others to snoop into."

A voice, clear and musical, filled the air. "They're nice people, Ian. I think we should all go inside for tea."

Sara stepped out from behind her husband. "I really have a wonderful tea. Ian brought it back from the market in Halifax. The tin has a picture of a Greek goddess with one of her . . ." She giggled and waved her hand vaguely in front of her chest. "You know, uncovered. Oh, but it's very classic. Come in." She skipped into the house.

Ian looked down at the ground. "I hope you take no offense to my words. I make no apologies for my need for privacy, and I ask you to respect that. Welcome to my home."

CHAPTER FOUR

Inside, a narrow set of stairs ascended to an upper landing. To the left was a dining room. Ian led them to a parlor on the right. Oil lamps hung from brackets on the walls, each with a polished reflector behind it. There were three chairs, all of different designs, a sofa, and two small tables. An unlit stone hearth sat on an inside wall near the center of the house. Several hooked rugs were scattered over wide floorboards.

Anna helped Sara with the tea while Ian took a large chair next to the hearth. The Talbots seated themselves on opposite sides of the room. Ian stared into the cold fireplace. No one spoke. Margaret cleared her throat. "You have a very lovely house, Mr. Grant."

Ian took the pipe from his mouth for an instant. "Yes."

"It is very old?"

"Yes."

She waited for him to continue. When he did not she asked, "Have you lived here long?"

"Yes."

Anna and Sara entered with a tea tray and cups. Sara poured with intense concentration and handed the cups around. "I had never had tea before Ian brewed it for me. It's so good. I have it every day now, several times a day. Ian brings me new tins when he goes to Halifax with Mr. Drummond. I keep them all when the tea is gone and fill them with sea shells that Ian brings me."

Sara spoke of the different shells she had and what creatures had inhabited them. Suddenly, the young woman leaped from the sofa. "Do you want to see my greatest treasure?"

Ian said, "I don't think the Talbots are interested."

"Of course they are, aren't you?"

Margaret said, "I'm certain it's very nice."

Sara clapped. "You see?" She took Margaret by the hand and ran to the stairs. At the top of the landing were two doors. She pushed open the right-hand door and dragged Margaret into a bedroom. The others followed.

Sara guided Margaret to a chest of drawers where shells of various colors and shapes were arranged on a bed of sand along with smooth chunks of wood draped with dried eel grass.

Sara carefully picked up one of the pieces of driftwood. "Ian brought it to me. Isn't it beautiful? Here, feel how the sea has polished it." She cradled the wood to her cheek and stroked it softly.

Ian leaned over and gently stroked her hair. She turned her head with the same look of youth and wonder in her eyes that had been captured in Thomas Brown's drawing.

They filed back downstairs where Margaret helped Anna and Sara clear the tea tray. The Grants had only one kitchen, located at the rear of the house just off the dining room. A wood-burning stove stood on one wall and a basin with a pump on another. Along other walls were cabinets, a pie safe, and a worktable with a marble top for rolling dough. A door led to the rear of the house. Two windows stood open.

When they came back into the parlor, Ian and John were carrying in the first trunk from the surrey. John wiped his forehead with a handkerchief. "This is one of Margaret's. Which room will she be sleeping in?"

Ian nodded his head toward the stairs. "Door on the left."

"Very well. And mine?"

Ian nodded toward the stairs a second time. "Door on the left."

Margaret gave a soft chuckle. "What my husband is referring to, Mr. Grant, is the room I will be sleeping in as opposed to the one he will be sleeping in."

"And what I'm referring to, Mrs. Talbot, is that there's one extra bedroom in this house and it has one bed where the both of you will be sleeping."

She stared at him for a moment before the meaning of his words collided within her. She had not slept in the same room with John, let alone the same bed, for two years.

There had been no discussion. John simply moved into another room after the stillbirth. At first she pleaded with him to return to her bed, to hold her against the terror of the night, to at least touch her hand. After a month she stopped pleading. After six she told herself it was better this way, to have no contact rather than yearn for something she could not have.

Pain throbbed behind her right eye at the thought of having him next to her, a hurtful reminder of what had once been and was no longer. This was followed by panic as she realized she would not be able to paint at night while he slept in another room.

Margaret forced a pleasant smile. "Surely, there must be another room somewhere."

Ian took the pipe out of his mouth. "If you're man and wife you only need but one bed." He paused and looked at John. "You are, aren't you?"

John squared his shoulders. "Of course we are."

"Then it's settled. Let's finish so Anna can get back."

When everything was unloaded, Anna put on her gloves. "Ian, you should show the Talbots your dock this morning."

"There's still plenty of time left for fishing today, even with interruptions."

"This is all settled. Mr. Talbot has promised to pay you for your time, isn't that right?"

John said, "That is my contract with the village. Everyone in Glasen will be fully compensated for any losses incurred, plus a ten percent bonus for being interviewed."

Ian struck a match with a sharp crack. "In that case we'd better get started, Mr. Talbot. This is costing you a pretty penny. Mrs. Talbot, Sara will help you unpack."

Sara's eyes widened. "Oh, yes, yes, yes." She took Margaret's hand again. "You can show me all your clothes, especially the underthings."

Margaret gently pulled her hand free. "I would love to show you my clothes later, but just now I need to go with the men and see your husband's tools so I can draw them."

Sara rolled her eyes. "Oh, you can see them anytime. Ian goes to the dock every day."

"Well, I have to go anyway. Mr. Talbot and I are a team."

John said, "Margaret's right. We work together on every article."

Sara lowered her head in a pout.

Ian tapped the bowl of his pipe. "I expect you know your business, Mr. Talbot. Well, let's go."

Anna adjusted her hat as she walked toward the front door. "I'll be back in the morning to take you in to see Father Williams." She walked outside and Margaret heard the clink of the harness.

Margaret took Sara's hand and smiled. "I promise to show you all of my clothes when we get back. Why don't you come with us down to the dock?"

Sara's eyes opened wide as her jaw trembled. She dropped Margaret's hands and stepped back slowly, shaking her head as she went. Ian bounded across the room and put his arms around her. She clung desperately to him. He kissed her gently on the forehead. "Go up and make certain your shells are all arranged proper, the way you like them. When we come back we can all play a game of cards. Would you like that?" She nodded, her face still pale, and went upstairs. Ian turned back to the Talbots with a scowl on his face. "Sara never goes near the sea."

Ian led them down a path next to bluffs that overlooked the Atlantic Ocean. Only the gentlest of waves lapped at a gravel beach. The sky, cloudless and deep blue, ran unbroken to the horizon.

A set of wooden stairs descended to a dock. On either side was a rocky beach. A shed was built on the dock off to one side. A dozen gulls huddled on its pitched roof. Others flew overhead and screeched as they soared or swooped down to the placid waters. Two dories were moored at the far end. The exteriors of their hulls were painted dark green and the interiors light buff. The rest of the wood, including the gunwales and oars, was covered in clear varnish.

The heat and humidity were already rising. Margaret fanned herself with the sketchbook. As she walked past the shed, she judged it to be perhaps eight feet wide and fifteen long, with a wide door.

John surveyed the ocean. "Is that a ship?"

Margaret strained to see the spot John pointed to, until she made out two masts with sails unfurled. Ian nodded. "That's Hugh Drummond and the *Lion*. She can only clear the shoals at high tide."

John made notes as they walked toward the shed. "What do you keep in here?"

Ian opened the door. "Supplies."

Margaret peeked inside. There were buckets, line, nets, buoys, lanterns, and a host of objects she could not identify. All were neatly arranged on shelves and wall hooks. She mechanically roughed out sketches of the contents as her mind searched for a place where she could paint in secret. She considered the shed, but that would require making Ian privy to her secret. Flora Brown might help if Margaret promised to show Thomas's work to the right people, but Thomas didn't seem to want anything to do with her after his seizure.

John walked out on the dock and looked down at the dories. "Five benches?"

"They're called thwarts, Mr. Talbot."

John made a note. "I see oars and a sail. Which do you use?"

"When there's a good breeze, I sail to the spot where I'll fish, otherwise I row."

John wrote in his unique shorthand. He looked to the shed. "You obviously can't row more than one boat at a time. Why isn't the other one stored in there?"

"If I were to take that dory out of the water, the wood would dry out and shrink. The boat wouldn't be watertight anymore."

Margaret lowered her sketchbook. "What kinds of fish do you catch, Mr. Grant?"

At first it seemed as if he hadn't heard her. He turned slowly and she prepared to hear a lecture on butting into a man's conversation. Instead, he pointed to the sea with his pipe. "There are halibut, haddock, sole, salmon, but this is the great breeding' ground of the Atlantic cod which is where the money is."

Ian tapped his pipe, lifted the top of a small barrel and pointed to a coiled line laden with barbed hooks. "Once I reach a spot I let out the line and trawl a bit. There's a hook every foot or so. Not every one's taken when I reel the line back in, but on a good day I'll haul in all the fish I can carry."

"Why does cod bring in the money?"

"It's dried cod that pays, Mrs. Talbot. Split and salted and dried in the sun, then pressed into barrels likes pages of a book. Prepared such it will stay unspoiled for months, even in tropical climates where most of it is shipped, boiled, and eaten."

"How often do you go out?"

For the first time he smiled at her. "How often does the sun rise? Except for Sunday, I go out every day, unless the weather beats me back. Then I stay ashore and make repairs. Fish don't take holidays."

"Didn't Sara say that you went to Halifax with Mr. Drummond?"

He laughed. "Now, if you've only come to draw pictures, I fear greatly the interrogation your husband will put me to."

Anger started to build in Margaret. "Excuse me, Mr. Grant. I was simply interested."

John stepped between them, "Please, sir, don't feel we are intruding."

Ian lit his pipe. "I didn't say I disliked the questions. I merely meant that they were very keen. Now, as to Hugh Drummond, I sail with him to Halifax every other month or so. He makes regular runs to sell our wares at a better price than we could get by ourselves. Two or three dory men accompany him on each trip."

Margaret closed her sketchbook. "I think I have enough for now. I'll go do some drawings of the house."

The men took no notice of her as she walked up the stairs. She made a perfunctory sketch of the house. It would pass if John asked to see what she was doing while he and Ian continued to talk.

She walked around the area. There was an outdoor well immediately behind the house that was hidden from the road. Further away was an outhouse. Margaret knew from having grown up with one on her family's farm that it was placed so as to leach away from the well and not contaminate the ground water. She remembered how her uncle from Georgia called it the *necessary room* when he visited.

On the other side of the main house was a barn-like structure with wide double doors that were secured with a lock. She looked through a window. Several trunks were stacked on shelves and a few were strewn across the floor. In the center of the floor stood a black carriage with two padded leather seats facing one another. There was a third bench up front for the driver, a fringed canopy, and lanterns on either side. Margaret had seen such carriages. They belonged to the wealthiest families. It must have cost Ian a year's earnings as a fisherman.

Behind the carriage was a great empty space of floor next to a window that faced out to sea and away from the house. There was more than enough room to set up her easel and supplies. She would have to paint in the morning instead of the evening.

Her mind set, she walked into the kitchen. Sara stood at the wash basin. She worked the handle of the indoor pump with one hand, while she immersed the other in the flow of water. Her eyes stared intently at the water cascading over her wrist and fingers as she hummed a tune that seemed both sad and sweet.

At Margaret's approach, Sara stopped and turned. She stared blankly for an instant, and then broke into laughter. "The men will be back in a moment and we have to set out the cards. Oh, this will be so much fun. We haven't played cards since Anna and Alistair were over last month."

Soon after, John and Ian tromped into the kitchen. The sound of the gulls resounded from outside. Ian closed the door and the din receded to the background.

A deck of playing cards sat on the table, along with a sheaf of paper and a pencil. Sara jumped up and down. "You're home, you're home." She ran and put her arms around Ian. He looked uncomfortably at Margaret and John before returning Sara's embrace. "Well, little one, what shall we play?"

"Oh, whist." She looked to Margaret and John. "You do play, don't you?"

Margaret said, "I've heard the name. It's like bridge, isn't it?"

"It's the best. Say you'll play, please."

John rubbed his jaw. "I used to play with my mother and some of her friends when I was young. I think I remember most of the rules."

Ian said, "Sara, dear, perhaps we should play a more modern game."

Margaret smiled. "Actually, I'd very much like to learn."

Sara squealed and clapped her hands.

Ian shrugged. "Very well. We usually cut the deck for partners, but as you're just learning, Mrs. Talbot, why don't you play with Sara and I'll be your partner, Mr. Talbot."

They sat at the table with partners directly across from each another. Ian shuffled the deck and dealt. It was the kind of game where everyone laid a card of the same suit face up on the table and the person whose card had the highest value gathered them together to count as a point, called a trick. "You can't talk about the game during play," said Ian, "But you can socialize. A good game of whist often has little to do with cards."

The deck was dealt face down. From bridge, Margaret understood the concepts of taking a trick and sluffing a card when you ran out of the lead suit. "Can you trump in whist?"

"Yes."

"How is the suit determined? Is there bidding?"

At this point Ian reached the last card of the deck and turned it face up on the table. It was the three of diamonds. "The last card dealt determines the trump suit. It's displayed on the table until the first trick is taken."

"Are there any other rules I should know?"

"Just one. Never trump your partner unless you have a very good reason for doing so. Many a marriage has fallen on hard times for the like. All right. Pick up your cards."

Margaret looked across the table to Sara. Her wild exuberance was replaced with earnest concentration. Sara slowly laid an ace of hearts on the table. They all laid down hearts. Sara gathered up the cards and stacked them in front of her.

Play continued. The lead fell to Margaret. The highest card in her hand was the ten of spades. The jack had not been played. There was only a one in three chance that Sara held it.

Margaret looked across the table and tried to glean some idea of what card to play. Sara's wide, dark eyes focused on her. Margaret stared back, trying to decide what to do. Sara remained motionless. It grew very quiet, and Margaret realized she could no longer hear the gulls outside. She could hear no sound at all. The room dimmed, except for Sara's eyes. Though the young woman's lips did not move, Margaret was certain she heard her say, "What have I played?"

Margaret shook her head. The room came into sharp focus. The muffled sound of gulls returned. She looked to Ian, avoiding Sara's glance, and back to John. "I'm sorry. I must have dozed off. Is it my play?"

John said, "Yes."

Margaret replayed the game in her mind. Sara had laid down a three of hearts the time before. That didn't tell her anything. The time before that, John had played the king of spades. She couldn't forget his snide grin. What had Sara played? A four? No. The queen. Margaret suppressed a smile as she laid her ten of spades on the table.

Ian triumphantly slapped the jack on it. Sara deftly trumped it with a six of diamonds.

As Sara took in the trick, she looked across the table with her lips turned up in a smile.

When the game was over, Margaret and Sara proved victorious. The spell of calm over Sara evaporated. She jumped up from the table, took Margaret by the hand, and led her into the kitchen. "It's time to prepare lunch. We'll have a soup of mussels and cod and herbs and potatoes. Potatoes are my new favorite. When I first came it was bread, all hard on the outside and soft on the inside like a lobster. Now, it's potatoes."

Sara combined fish heads, fins, shell fish, sea weed, and things Margaret could not identify. She didn't think she would be able to eat the concoction and keep it down. Sara stirred and tasted, adding ingredients as she went. "This will be very good."

Margaret remained silent.

At the table, Margaret held her spoon over the bowl of chowder. In her travels she had downed many wretched meals which were considered local delicacies. Her general rule for survival in a foreign land was to eat all of whatever you were given, smile, thank your host, and explain how you are just too full for more.

She looked over at Sara, who stared back silently. With a deep breath, Margaret plunged the spoon into the chowder, drew up a large portion and stuffed it in her mouth.

It was the most delightful thing she had ever tasted. The flavor was sweet and spicy, salty and bitter, rich and delicate all at the same time. She closed her eyes for a moment. When she opened them again Sara was giggling. "You thought it was going to taste terrible, didn't you? I could tell."

Margaret said, "I was just expecting..." She stopped, trying to think up a story to save her dignity. She shook her head and smiled. "Yes. I thought it was going to taste terrible." Everyone at the table laughed, including John.

After lunch, Ian went out to sea in his dory. Phillip arrived with the trunk containing Blossom's portrait hidden inside. Sara kept him half an hour for tea. Margaret unpacked, making certain to keep the painting concealed. Sara did some chores around the house before going out to the garden.

Ian returned just before sunset and they had another delicious meal of fish and bread and carrots. Afterwards, they all sat in the parlor. John patted his stomach. "I don't know when I've eaten better."

Ian lit his pipe. "My Sara is the greatest of all cooks. Just one of her many marvelous qualities."

Sara's face brightened. "Do you really think so?"

He put out his match. "I do indeed."

She leaped from the sofa and put her arms around him. "Isn't he the grandest?" She nuzzled her head into his chest. Ian gently stroked Sara's hair.

John cleared his throat. "It's been years since I played whist. We'll have to teach it to our friends."

Ian gazed across the room. "The old things still have some worth, even in this new century."

John said, "How do you think the twentieth century will change Glasen, Mr. Grant?"

He took his pipe from his mouth. "Much as it will anywhere else. People will be born. People will die. Some will grow fat and some will starve. People here are not that much different than in New York when it comes to changing centuries, Mr. Talbot.

"I lived in New York, Mr. Talbot. I've been to London. I've been to Paris and many other places. Each is different. Each has its flavor, its greatness, and its stupidities. When it all comes down to it, everyone's just trying to live the best they can." He took a long draw on his pipe. "People in Glasen are no different."

Margaret looked to Sara. "Did you go on these travels with Ian?"

Her eyes darted between Margaret and Ian. "I traveled here."

"Oh, I see. Where do you come from?"

Ian pulled Sara closer to him. "Never ask that again, Mrs. Talbot. I've it made it clear my privacy will be respected."

John said, "My wife meant no harm, Mr. Grant."

Margaret stood up. "I can speak for myself. John. Mr. Grant, I apologize if I have intruded on your privacy. I was merely curious and, as such, asked a question that would be considered perfectly normal in polite society. Perhaps you should give us a written list of subjects not to be discussed."

Ian moved Sara to one side and stood, his frame towering above Margaret. "I am not accustomed to having my manners questioned in my own home."

Margaret took a step toward him, her head raised to meet his eyes. "And I am not accustomed to being insulted by my hosts."

"Everyone sit down." Sara's voice was sharply penetrating. Margaret found herself in her chair again—though she could not explain how she'd gotten there. Ian sat on the sofa. Sara remained still. "It's been a long day. We should go to sleep. In the morning we will feel much better."

Ian rubbed his eyes. "Again, I am forced to apologize. Your question was perfectly natural and I had no right to speak as I did."

Margaret felt a deep blush come to her whole face. "I apologize for my rudeness. I don't know what came over me." She was surprised at how light the admission made her feel. She looked at Ian and they spontaneously laughed.

Margaret and John went upstairs, put on their nightclothes and got into bed without touching each other. The window was wide open, but the air in the room was still stifling. There was no moon and once the oil lamp was extinguished, the bedroom was totally dark.

Margaret whispered, "What do you think of our hosts?"

John fluffed his pillow. "Ian is all right, once you get past that tough fisherman act. He's got something to hide, though."

"Something to hide, or someone to protect. It all centers on Sara and her odd behavior. Do you remember that tall, young man who was at Jill's party?"

"The one from Vienna?"

"Yes. He mentioned a book that was published in Germany last year by a neurologist named Freud. It describes people like Sara, calm one moment, uncontrollable the next. The author calls the condition hysteria and says it can be an expression of sexual repression or abuse. Something must have happened to her when she was young, something that was so shocking she spends all her waking hours hiding it."

"And you think Ian is trying to protect her? That could account for his reaction when we ask about Sara's past. Perhaps he's worried we'll dig up whatever it is she's terrified of and that it will drive her mad."

Margaret said, "That could be. But, perhaps he's afraid of something else. This Dr. Freud has his patients relive their fears in order to confront and release them. This seems to cure the hysteria."

"In that case, Ian should be delighted."

"Unless he's afraid that once the terror is removed, Sara won't need him anymore."

The sound of an owl woke Margaret in the middle of the night. For a moment she wasn't certain where she was. It seemed like her own room in New York where she slept alone. The window was in the right place, as was the door. John's room would be down the hall.

But it wasn't her room, and John lay curled up asleep next to her with his arm slung inadvertently across her waist. She felt the slow, rhythmic swells of his breathing, heard the soft, almost silent whoosh of air in and out of his lungs, and inhaled that fragrance that was uniquely John Talbot.

She let herself forget the last two years and fell back to a time when they did sleep together and held each other at night. She told herself she was a fool. The pain would return when she awoke again to his cold withdrawal in the morning. *Move away from him*, she told herself. *Don't let illusion bring pain.*

She closed her eyes and left his arm tucked around her.

CHAPTER FIVE

Margaret awoke to the soft light of an overcast morning. John lay asleep next to her. His face, usually taut these last two years, was relaxed and peaceful. The memory of his arm around her waist in the middle of the night left a phantom warmth.

She got out of bed carefully, afraid to wake him and lose the moment. The fragrance of pancakes seeped through the bedroom door as she got dressed. John mumbled something in his sleep. She turned around to see his arm reach out for the place where she had been lying only moments before. She left the window open, but pulled the curtains to let John sleep a little longer.

Though there had been a rain shower during the night that broke the oppressive heat, she knew it would return by the afternoon. Thoughts of the Glasen Hotel and its now-destroyed baths came to her as she dreaded the humidity. Ian and Sara had to have some sort of bathing facilities. She hoped it wasn't the ocean.

Her mind focused on the problem of where she could hide her studio. She carefully parted the bedroom curtain and examined the locked carriage house. It was perfect. Could Sara be trusted to help her get inside without telling Ian or John? She closed the curtains and slipped downstairs.

In the kitchen, Sara busily cooked breakfast on the wood stove. Three plates sat on the marble pastry table. Each was filled to overflowing with pancakes. Margaret stared at the excess of food, far more than the four of them could eat.

The thump of shoes resounded down the stairs. John entered the dining room and Margaret smiled.

The serene face John had born in sleep was gone. He sat down at the table without looking at her. "Why didn't you wake me?"

She took a step back, her fingers intertwined across her belly. "I thought you would want to rest. It was a long trip."

"We're already behind schedule. Kindly leave the curtains open from now on so the sun will rouse me."

A knock came at the front door. Sara ran from the kitchen and through the dining room. In a moment she skipped back into the dining room with Anna Lamont in tow. Sara clapped her hands. "I'm so happy to see you. Come sit down and have some breakfast. I made a few pancakes." She ran back into the kitchen.

Anna shook her head. "How many has she made?"

Before Margaret could reply, Sara was back in the dining room, placing plates of pancakes on the table. "Eat all you want. I can always make more."

They sat down and ate, even Anna. Margaret placed a single pancake on her plate, poured some maple syrup over it and took a bite. It dissolved in her mouth. A sweet honey-and-nut flavor spread across her tongue as she let slip a pleasurable moan. "Oh, Sara, these are magnificent."

Sara shrieked with glee. "Ian said I shouldn't try anything new on guests, but I was certain you'd like them. I've never cooked them before. I ate them once at Mrs. Larson's, but Ian never asks for them, so I've never made them."

"Well, I will have to thank Mrs. Larson for teaching you."

"She didn't teach me. I just remembered how they tasted and made them up, though I changed a few things."

Margaret finished the pancake on her plate and unashamedly took another. She usually ate a light breakfast, disliking the bloated feeling of being too full when starting her day. Sara's cooking left her satisfied yet never overfull, no matter how much she ate. "Isn't Ian going to join us?"

Sara laughed. "Silly. Ian went out to sea before dawn. He'll not be home till supper."

Anna stood up from the table. "We should be going too. Can't keep Father Williams waiting."

The ride into the village was quiet. Anna asked how they were settling in and Margaret replied that everything was fine. A few more questions from Anna met with polite but quick answers by Margaret. John said nothing.

At the church, a stained glass window with the image of a dove in flight was set above the door. A steeply pitched roof with a high steeple rose over the building.

Inside, more stained glass windows lined the walls. One showed the raising of Lazarus, another the act of the Good Samaritan, still another the absolution of the woman caught in adultery.

Fr. Williams walked into the sanctuary through a door beside the altar. "Mr. and Mrs. Talbot. Anna. How good to see all of you."

Anna said, "Well, here they are, delivered safe and sound." She looked back to Margaret and John. "Just come over to the house whenever you're ready to go back."

The Talbots followed Fr. Williams into his office. The walls were lined with bookshelves. Four chairs faced a large desk behind which hung a copy of El Greco's *The Crucifixion*.

Margaret got out her sketchbook and charcoal. "I hope I may draw you while we speak."

"Mrs. Talbot, to be your subject is an honor."

John opened a notebook. "Let's begin with your assignment to this Parish."

Margaret sketched with gray and white charcoal pencils as she half listened to the interview. She found it helped her understand her subjects better and allowed her to bring out their true characters in her drawings. John continued asking questions about fishermen and blessing the fleet and births and deaths. Even when they fought, even when they could barely speak to each other, Margaret always felt a quickening excitement when she heard John's voice guide a subject in search of what that person really thought or felt. He was the best, and she took pride in that.

Someone knocked at the door. Fr. Williams said, "Come in."

A young man, no more than twenty, stuck his head into the room. "Excuse me, Father. Kathleen and I were wonderin' if we could talk to you abou' the mass."

A young woman's voice came from the hallway in a hushed whisper. "James, he's busy. We'll come back later."

James looked back into the hallway, then to Fr. Williams, then to the hallway again, then back to Fr. Williams. "It's just that Aunt Ruth changed her mind again abou' the headstone and her and mom are fightin' over what to do with his sawmill and it don't seem right to the memory o' poor Uncle Gordon and ..." He looked back into the hall. "Well ...we'll come back later."

Fr. Williams stood up. "You'll do no such thing. Come inside, both of you. I'd like you to meet our guests from America."

James entered the room. Margaret noticed that he twisted his cap the same way Thomas Brown did. A young woman with dark hair followed. She was pregnant and nearly to term.

Fr. Williams said, "John and Margaret Talbot, I would like to introduce James and Kathleen Myers. It was my pleasure to marry them last year."

The priest took Kathleen by the hand and led her to one of the chairs. He sat back behind the desk. "I know this is hard for the two of you."

James nodded. "Sometimes I think that Kathleen and I are the only ones who cared abou' Uncle Gordon." He looked to John. "My dad was drowned when I was eight. Uncle Gordon was pretty much a father to me from that time on."

Fr. Williams said, "Are you going to take over the sawmill? I know your uncle wanted you to."

Kathleen's face brightened. James twisted his cap. "Mom wants to sell it and use the money to move to Montreal. She says she's tired of fish and forests and wants to live in the city and ride on street cars. We'll eventually get something from the sale, but we need money to live on now. That's why I've signed on with Mr. Drummond and the *Lion*. I'll be shipping out when he returns. I'm afraid if mom and auntie don't stop bickering I'll be gone for the funeral mass and Kathleen will be left to deal with them alone."

Fr. Williams came around the desk and placed his hands on James' shoulders. "You've always taken on the full load of a man and God sees your strength. I'll go around this afternoon and have a talk with your mother and your aunt. This is no time for them to be feuding."

"Thank you, Father."

"We'll have the mass before Hugh puts out again. It's only fair to you. Don't worry. God works in mysterious ways. You two go off and spend some time together."

James shook John's hand. "I'm pleased to meet you, Mr. Talbot. We're all very excited over your article."

"It was nice to meet you," said Margaret. "Are you hoping for a boy or a girl?"

Kathleen covered her belly as if to hide the pregnancy and gave a nervous smile. James escorted her out.

Margaret said, "Did I say something wrong, Father?"

Fr. Williams sat back down. "I do not know why this is, but when a woman gets in a family way around here, everyone ignores it. I have watched families posing for a photograph in which an expecting wife will stand behind someone else to conceal her condition. I'm not certain if this is because so many children die young that there is the wish to be detached, or if there is a fear of placing a curse for boasting."

For an instant, Margaret's mind was back in the hospital with the doctors and nurses shouting frantically. Could she have avoided the feelings of despair and loss had she remained cold and detached?

She made several sketches. John continued his interview. From experience, she knew he might continue on for another hour or more.

"Father, it has been a pleasure to capture your image. I hope I may trouble you for another sitting before we leave."

"You could not possibly be a trouble, Mrs. Talbot."

"Thank you. If you'll excuse me John, I think I'll go down to the wharf for some drawings and then to the Lamont's house."

It was only slightly muggy as Margaret walked toward the wharf. Still, she felt the press of moist air against her as she noticed several men stripped down to their undershirts. Her own long-sleeved blouse was buttoned at the neck and rubbed against the sweat on her skin as she envied the men for another privilege they alone enjoyed.

She noticed the same brick and wooden buildings she had seen when they first arrived in Glasen. They would make good subjects for her sketches. There were less than a dozen workers at the wharf, all of them very young or very old. Those who were able were out to sea, fishing, or in the woods cutting timber. Margaret walked inside the brick building. Shafts of light filtered from high windows to cast pools of illumination across the floor.

Tackle hung from the walls. A large pile of white material sparkled crystalline in a bin in one corner. Margaret assumed it was the salt they used to preserve the fish.

Two dories sat upside down on wooden braces. Men wearing leather aprons stood next to the boats. They used tools with long wooden handles and metal blades to scrape the hulls in long, rhythmic movements. One man appeared to be in his sixties, the other in his twenties. Margaret sat on a crate, opened her sketchbook, and began drawing. She played with the image of the men in bright contrast to the dark background.

The scrape of metal on wood echoed through the large space. When she finished the first sketch, she walked toward the boats to see more detail. The younger man followed her with his eyes as she drew closer. He placed his scraping tool on the boat and turned away. Margaret was close enough to see that the young man was Thomas Brown.

He ran for a back door. Margaret quickly followed. "Thomas. Wait."

Thomas charged through the door. Margaret was there an instant later. The opening led to a narrow section of wharf. Margaret ran back into the brick building and out the front door. She caught Thomas coming around from the other side.

He stared at her. "Well, go ahead. Laugh. You've gone to enough trouble to find me."

Margaret said, "Why should I laugh?"

He stepped back. "It's pretty funny, isn't it? The freak who can't work on the sea has to scrape boats with the old men."

Margaret opened her sketchbook. "I've been working on a portrait of Father Williams today. Have you drawn anything since I last saw you?"

"I don't draw anymore." His body started to shake. Margaret moved toward him. He crossed his arms over his chest. "If you're waiting for another performance, I'm afraid you'll be disappointed today. I don't get excited anymore, either."

She threw the sketchbook to the wharf and placed her hands on her waist. "Stop it!"

Thomas stepped back.

Margaret said, "You listen to me, Thomas Brown. We all have to face the world with the problems life gives us. I have problems. Mr. Talbot has problems. Phillip Lamont has problems. Ian Grant has problems. We all do. I don't have time for your self-pity, and neither do you. Now, do you want to become an artist, or do you want to sit in this village and complain for the rest of your life about what you could have been?"

Thomas opened his mouth, and closed it again.

Margaret remained silent. Overhead, gulls screeched as they floated in the breeze in search of fish. The fleet would not return for hours, but the birds still waited diligently.

Thomas closed his eyes. "I'm afraid."

Margaret softened her voice. "Let's step around to the back of the building."

Thomas nodded. She picked up the sketchbook and he followed her to a narrow alleyway between the buildings. Margaret checked to make certain they were alone. "Thomas, you have phenomenal talent, but you must learn how to use it."

He scuffed his boots on the wharf. "What good would it do? I'll never leave this village."

"Why? Because you have epilepsy? Thomas, do you know who Julius Caesar was?"

"Of course. I went to school. What does he have to do with anything?"

"Julius Caesar became the most powerful man of his time, and he was epileptic."

Thomas looked down at his feet. "Don't make jokes like that."

"It's true, Thomas. You're not the first person to have epilepsy. So, do you want to be an artist?"

Tears formed in his eyes. "Yes."

Margaret placed her hand on his shoulder. "I'm going to work on my sketches all day tomorrow at the Grants' house. Can you come see me at noon?"

"Will Mr. Talbot be there?"

"No. He'll be in the village."

Thomas bit his lower lip. "It wouldn't look proper."

"Sara will be there. No one will gossip if she's in the house, will they?"

"I suppose not."

"Then you'll come?"

He looked at her for a long while. "I'll be there."

There was a conviction in his eyes that reflected her own joy and passion for painting. Her time with him would be short, but she would guide him as best she could. All she had to do was make certain John did not find out about the lesson. He might tolerate her taking some time away from the article to show Thomas how to draw, but Margaret intended to teach her new student how to paint in oils.

Thomas returned to his work. Margaret heard the scuffing of feet and turned to find Beth Ramsey staring at her. The short, chubby woman still wore a shawl over her gray hair and black lace mittens on her hands.

She raised a finger to Margaret. "Well, witch. Corruptin' our youth, I see."

Margaret tried to walk around her.

Beth Ramsey thrust a crucifix toward Margaret. "Not so quick, witch. I would have words with ye."

"I am not a witch, and I'll thank you to stop calling me that."

"I saw you defile our sanctuary and bewitch the priest. Be warned. I'm watchin' both you and that sprite that bewitched Ian."

Margaret had encountered religious zealots before, but never one like Beth Ramsey. Everything the woman said made no sense. "Are you talking about Sara?"

"As well you know, witch. You'll show your true nature soon enough, and when you do, I'll tie the both of you to stakes and burn you. Then back to the De'il you'll go, to burn for eternity in hell."

Beth Ramsey backed out of the alley and around the corner with the crucifix held like a shield.

Margaret's hands were still shaking when she arrived at the Lamont's house. Anna greeted her at the door with a smile.

"And how was your day, dear?"

"Good and bad."

Anna's smile changed to a frown. "What's the matter?"

"I just had a conversation with Beth Ramsey."

Anna shook her head. "Oh, that woman. Well, you better come in and sit down."

Anna guided Margaret into a parlor adorned with blue-and-white striped wallpaper. The ceiling had an ornate medallion in the center where a gas jet would be—if Glasen had town gas. Instead, kerosene lamps were placed on tables and in holders on the walls. Margaret settled into a cushioned sofa, and Anna sat in a chair next to her. "Now, tell me what happened."

Margaret relayed the encounter in full, with the exception of having spoken with Thomas. When she described Beth Ramsey's threat to burn her and Sara alive, the hairs on her neck stood up. As she talked, she began to wonder if it was safe for Thomas to come out to the Grants' house.

Margaret realized her hands had stopped shaking. "I'm probably overreacting a little, but she was so maniacal."

"I'll have Phillip go over and talk to her. She's the kind of person who needs to be sat on every once in a while. But don't be too upset. She can rile folks up for a while, but doesn't hold much sway when push comes to shove. You sit here and rest. I'll get us something cool to drink."

"Thank you. That would be very nice."

Anna left for a moment and returned with a tray containing a pitcher of lemonade with ice floating on top.

Margaret accepted her glass and took a long drink. "This is so good, Anna. The ice is the best part. Thank you."

"My pleasure, dear. You can thank Alistair for that. He started cutting ice from the frozen lakes and storing it in vaults beneath the ground the winter after the store opened. The Lamonts have been supplying ice to the whole area ever since."

"I didn't expect this kind of heat here. It was cooler in Africa where John and I were four summers ago."

"Africa? That must have been exciting."

"It was the most amazing place I've ever been. Not at all what I expected. We stayed with a tribe whose women give birth squatting rather than lying down. The mothers said they feel almost no pain and labor took a third as long. I watched such a birth, but we'll never be able to use the sketches I made." That trip had been before the stillbirth. Was it possible that her own baby would have lived had she given birth that way?

The two women sipped the tart liquid. Just as Margaret wished she had a fan, Anna produced two from some unseen place and handed one to her. With the glass in one hand and the fan waving in another, Margaret leaned back against the sofa and tried to think of winter snow. As she did, it settled on her just how tired she was. The two days they had been in Glasen seemed like a week.

Anna refilled their glasses from the pitcher. "How are you getting along with the Grants?"

Anna's question came filtering past the lemonade and the cool breeze across her face from the fan. A part of her wished she could ignore it and fall further into the cushions of the sofa, and another part was glad to have the thought of Beth Ramsey pushed aside.

"To tell you the truth," said Margaret, "I'm not sure how we're getting along. Ian's been helpful, but we've had a few arguments."

"Abou' Sara, I imagine."

"Mostly, yet she's the one who breaks the tension. It's just hard to be upset around her."

Anna said, "You look perplexed, dear."

Margaret took a deep breath. "I'm worried, Anna. There's something in Sara's past that brings out her strange behavior. I'm certain Ian knows what it is, even if she doesn't."

Anna nodded her head. "I don't pretend to know where Sara came from or what she's up to half the time. Lord knows Alistair and I have talked abou' it enough the last few years. But, I'm not certain it matters too much. It's plain that Sara loves Ian with all her soul, and Ian loves her just as deeply. She's the best thing that ever happened to him, and there's naught but the hand of God can separate them."

They sat in silence for a moment. Margaret took another sip of lemonade, deciding if she could trust Anna. "I talked to Thomas Brown today."

"Did you? I'd have thought the lad wouldn't want to speak to you or your husband."

"He didn't at first. I told him I wanted to see more of his work."

"What did he say?"

"He agreed to take some lessons from me before I leave."

"I'm so happy to hear that. The boy has always had talent."

"Anna, I don't want to ask you to lie, but please don't mention this to John. He sometimes gets irritated if he thinks I'm becoming distracted from an article."

Anna gave a wink. "It will be our secret, dear. If everything we ever concealed from our husbands was a lie, neither of us would ever get out of purgatory."

Margaret laughed and the tension she felt earlier drained away. She could not explain why, but she liked Anna and had the feeling she could tell her anything.

"So how are you getting along with the article?" Anna asked.

Margaret described John's activities over the past two days, his talks with Ian, his interview with Fr. Williams, his schedule for the article, and his plans for the next one.

When she was done, Anna leaned forward. "I hope you don't think I'm prying, dear, but the two of you aren't getting along well, are you?"

The question shocked Margaret. She tried to form a polite denial, but looking into Anna's eyes she couldn't bring herself to lie. Her own eyes teared over and she gave a deep sigh. Anna sat down next to her and handed her a handkerchief.

Margaret found herself telling Anna things she had never said to anyone, not even to her closest friends. She spoke of the passion that burned inside her to paint and to be recognized for her work, along with the fear that she would know neither. "I don't understand why John fights me so. I used to think he was jealous, but sometimes it's like he's afraid of me painting."

Haltingly, the story of the stillbirth came out. "I still think of the baby that I couldn't hold. I don't even know if it was a boy or a girl. They acted like it was a tooth being pulled. I thought I had done something to kill my baby and I wanted to die, too."

She told Anna how John had turned cold toward her even before she left the hospital, and how she held a pillow close to her at night as if it were him. "I don't know if he's punishing me for killing the baby, or if he just hates me."

All the while, Anna sat silently next to her.

Margaret dabbed her eyes. "I'm so sorry to have bothered you."

"Oh, hush. We'll have none of that. To begin with, you didn't kill your baby. Many a women here and abou' has lost a child at birth. There's no evil in it and no blame. Do you understand?"

Margaret nodded her head. "It all happened after the hospital. Things have been so bad. All we do is argue, and I can't understand how it happens. I really can't."

"It wouldn't have anything to do with the two of you being a little headstrong, would it?"

Margaret laughed. "Well, I guess you could say that. Sometimes it's as bad as having my eyebrows plucked to let him win an argument. He just gets so smug about it. And then he wants to lecture me, like I was some kind of idiot. It makes me so…oh." She clenched her fist, searching for the right word.

"I know, dear. It's galling how they can be sometimes, like no one could have ever have an idea before they did."

"That's it. And I know John doesn't really think I'm stupid, but he still treats me that way, as if I was a child. Anna, I've created works of art that have taken people's breath away—real art, not just the illustrations for the magazines. He won't even talk about them. If it's not about the articles, he just doesn't care."

Anna sat back and fanned herself for a moment. "He may have a lot on his mind and doesn't notice how important painting is to you."

"But how can he be so callous? He's a writer. He's supposed to notice things."

"And how much do you notice? What does your husband want from life? Fame? Money? Success?"

The door opened and Alistair tromped in. "Just been down to the store. That new bolt of fabric should be in by week's end." He stopped when he saw Margaret. "Well, good afternoon, Mrs. Talbot. It's a pleasure to see you again. How has your stay been?"

"Very nice, thank you."

Anna looked up at him. "Alistair?"

He looked back with the slightest nod of his head. "Well, at the sake of being rude, I must excuse myself. Call me when tea's ready." He quickly left the room.

Margaret stared after him. "John would have wanted to know everything that was going on before he left, and he still wouldn't have taken a hint."

"And how well do you take a hint? I nearly had to hit you over the head with a tea tray at Phillip Lamont's house to get you out of that pit you'd dug yourself into."

Margaret felt the burn of a blush.

Anna said, "There's an old saying around here, *two deaf geese will squawk forever*. When was the last time you asked your husband what he wanted?"

"It's obvious what he wants. Illustrations for the articles."

"But did you ask him? Directly? He might want something else entirely, and you just think you know."

"If he wanted something don't you think he'd tell me? Is it my job to interrogate him? I've tried. After losing the baby I asked and pleaded to know what he felt. All I can figure is he never wanted the baby because he's never said a blessed thing. How could he not say something? We fight constantly but we never talk about anything."

Anna paused as if making a decision. "Now, dear, I'm going to admit something to you that no living person other than Alistair knows. When I was a young girl I was rather headstrong. Well, wild might be a better description. If you'd told me the sea was blue I'd argue it was green. I just couldn't stand anyone being right but myself.

"Alistair, too, was a bit stubborn. We had the most terrible arguments abou' the most foolish things, and it's a wonder we ever got to the kirk. But get there we did, and the holy sacraments spoken, and there we were, not yet twenty, poor as the mice in the steeple, and too proud to blow our noses.

"Alistair took to the sea, as with most men on Caribou Island, and we'd settled in a shack near the water. It was cold and damp and the wind blew through the cracks in the wall. We'd argue and bicker until one morning we had our worst fight ever. I can't even remember what it was abou', but I recall how I'd said I was leaving him for good. 'Fine', he'd said to me. 'Just don't go takin' the big kettle.'

"I think he said that just to be spiteful because it was terribly heavy and Alistair must have thought I couldn't lift it. It sat on a hook over the hearth and I'd used it to make the fish broth we lived on.

"Well, so obstinate was I that I'd poured the stock out onto the coals, wrestled it out of the shack, filled it with my clothes, and marched over to my mother's house, dragging the kettle behind. When I got there, she looked at me, looked at my clothes, and looked longest at the kettle. I'd told her how I couldn't take Alistair's horrible abuse anymore and had left him. 'Anna,' says she. 'Home is where you should be.' I'd started up the steps and she said, 'This is not your home. Your home is with the man you married, for good or ill, and if you didn't marry him for good than the greater fool are you.'

"I couldn't believe her at first. When I saw she was serious, I pleaded and threatened, but it did no good. I wasn't comin' in. I could either sleep on the street or go back to the shack.

"Broken, I dragged that heavy kettle back, acutely aware that the neighbors were all staring. At one time I would have thrown my head back high and ignored them. That time, their stares burned into me. As I walked away, my mother called out to me, 'Anna. Remember. Perfect love canna be without equality, and the greatest equalizer is respect.'"

She gave a short laugh and smiled. "That night, Alistair came in, all sheepish, and handed me a small strip of lace that would fit around the collar of my dress. I knew he must have spent his whisky money on it. All arguments were forgotten abou'.

"Do you mean you never fought again?"

"I dinna say that. We've had quite a few disagreements over the years, and still have from time to time. But that night, we promised we would never again fight to hurt each other and to always listen. That was nearly fifty years ago. We've both kept our word ever since."

There was a knock at the door. Anna got up and let John in. Margaret made certain all traces of tears were wiped from her eyes before he entered the parlor.

John sat in a high-back chair across from Margaret.

Anna offered John some lemonade. "And how was your interview, Mr. Talbot?"

"Excellent. Father Williams is a delightful man."

Alistair came in. "I thought I heard your voice, Mr. Talbot. How was your day?"

John fell into his lecture mode as he relayed points of the interview, ending with an account of James and Kathleen Myers. "It was very sad to hear of his uncle's death."

Alistair said, "That poor lad's been the provider for his mother since he was eight, as well as the padding between her and his aunt."

Anna said, "Well, I imagine you'd like a ride back to the Grants' house. Shall we?"

CHAPTER SIX

Margaret lay awake most of the night as Anna's story rolled through her mind. She admitted to herself that she could be prideful and stubborn. Yet, John had withdrawn from her. She had asked him for affection and told him she needed to paint, but wasn't certain if she'd ever asked him what he wanted.

At sunrise, John stirred and got out of bed without a word. As he dressed, Margaret remained still and watched him through half-open eyelids. Without a glance at her, he left the room and descended the stairs with a thump-thump rhythm. She heard a knock downstairs followed by Anna's voice. "Good morning Mr. Talbot."

"Good morning, Anna."

"Is Margaret ready?"

"She's staying here to rework some material."

"Oh, I see."

The front door closed. Margaret stared at the ceiling and thought about the day. There were several drawings to change from rough sketches to finished illustrations, and Thomas Brown would be there at noon. Still, she remained under the sheets with no desire to move.

It was years of discipline that got her out of bed and dressed. The first thing she had to do was find Sara and ask her to open the carriage house so she could move her painting and the art supplies into it before Thomas arrived.

Margaret walked downstairs. "Sara? Are you here?" She looked through the rest of the house. Sara was nowhere to be found. Hunger rumbled in her stomach, but she decided to go outside and look for Sara before getting any breakfast.

There was no one at the dock where the second dory was moored. She opened the door to the shed and stepped inside. The only light came from the door. There were no windows. It would never do as a studio. She had to get into the carriage house.

A smaller set of stairs led down to the rocky beach. The scene was promising for a sketch, so she walked down and along the shore. It was so different from the sandy beaches near her childhood home in New Jersey. She looked for shells but saw none. Her grandmother would not have liked that. Margaret had often walked with her in search of shells and seaweed, though her mother disapproved and said it was a waste of time. Margaret wished her Grammy were still alive. She'd always listened to Margaret's problems and calmed her with just a few words. Her mind fell back to the time she had received her first rejection letter from a publisher. She'd sent portfolios to five newspapers and three magazines with her best work. Robert Henri had personally helped her select them. Each cover letter was proudly signed, "Margaret Cooper."

It had started as a fine summer morning on their farm. Margaret was just nineteen. She was sitting in the parlor with her mother and grandmother, mending socks. Her mother, Prudence, looked out the window to the road and said, "Mail's here. I'll get it." When she came back in she sorted through the letters and stopped with a slight frown on her face.

"This one's for you, Margaret."

Margaret gingerly took the envelope in her hand and read the return address. "Oh my. It's from one of the publishers. Oh my."

Her grandmother smiled. "Well open it, Margie."

"Yes." She fumbled with the envelope in her hand while still breathing in short gasps. "Oh my." She handed the letter to her grandmother. "You open it, Grammy. Read it to me."

"All right, dear." She opened the envelope and took out the letter. "Dear Miss Cooper, thank you for allowing us to review your material." She stopped and looked up at Margaret. "That's good."

Margaret wrung her hands together. Her grandmother continued reading. "Though we find your work interesting, it does not fit our current needs. We wish you the best in your illustrating career. Sincerely…" Her grandmother's voice trailed off.

Margaret stood silent for a moment. Her grandmother put the letter aside. "Oh, Margie. I am so sorry."

Her mother continued to darn socks. "I appreciate you wanting to help out and make some money, but you're never going to get into that world. It's men and only men. They saw your name and probably didn't even look at your work. That's how they are and the sooner you learn that the better off you'll be. Get a job suitable for a woman. You're going to get married to someone anyway and then you'll hardly have time for chores and children. Go out to Missouri or Ohio. Find a man with a shop where you can have a future. Get away from the sea and all this nonsense."

"Prudence, this is only the first letter," her grandmother said. "There are seven more to come. Let her see what they have to say."

"Do you really think someone will want my drawings, Grammy?"

"Of course someone will. You're very talented."

Prudence put down her darning. "Don't go filling the girl's head with nonsense. It was all right to take her along the beach and collect seashells when she was seven, but she has to face the facts of the world. She's nineteen and not even a beau. Do you want her to be an old maid at twenty-five?"

Her grandmother pointed her finger at her mother. "It's not fluff and you know it. You made your choice, as she will one day."

Margaret got up and ran from the room in tears. She didn't know where she was going, but she made her way to the beach with the waves rolling in and out. Her mother had never approved of the stories and songs her grandmother had taught her. She could never remember them right, anyway. She tried to convince herself that this was just one rejection and one of the others would lead to a life of illustrating. Another part of her mind was relieved at the rejection. She was trained in painting and that is the life she wanted. Maybe her mother was right. She should get married to a man who would support her, and allow her the time to just paint. It would be an easy way out.

The thought did not settle well. It had the tinge of betrayal and violated Robert Henri's teachings of being honest with the subject. She knew she had to go on and try.

It took a week for the last of the replies to come. All polite rejections. At each one, Margaret hardened and became more determined. Her mother acted as if the matter was closed.

That night, Margaret knocked on her grandmother's door. The elderly woman was in her bed clothes. She welcomed Margaret inside and closed the door.

"Grammy, I've been thinking about what mother said. Maybe it was my name that caused those editors to reject me."

Her grandmother brow furrowed. "Have you abandoned your dreams then, Margie?"

"Not at all. I'm going to send out a new batch of letters and sign them, 'M. Cooper.' This way they will look at my work."

"What will happen when they meet you?"

"At least they'll see what I can do."

Her grandmother thought for a moment. "You can't do this from here, Margie."

"You don't think the plan will work?"

"It will work. But you have to go where the publishers are. New York. You will need to meet people who can be helpful and be prepared for any opportunity."

"I can't afford that."

Her grandmother got up and walked to her dresser. The top was strewn with seashells the two of them had collected over the years. She opened a drawer and took out a small wooden box.

"This is for you, my dearest granddaughter."

Margaret opened the box and found hundreds of dollars. "I can't take this, Grammy. It should be used to help the family. That's why I wanted to illustrate."

"This is mine, saved over decades for a special occasion. This is that occasion. Go to New York."

Margaret touched the bills. "You talked about a choice I would make. Is this it?"

Her grandmother smiled. "This is a choice. There is another to come."

Margaret found a boarding house for women in Manhattan. She used master copies of her work to reproduce a new portfolio. They were all signed M. Cooper. Within three days she received an invitation to meet with an editor.

She tucked her portfolio under her arm and proceeded to the second floor of the editor's building. A woman with white hair sat behind a desk. She looked up. "Do you have an appointment?"

"I'm M. Cooper. I'm here to see Mr. Ross."

The woman got up, knocked on a sturdy, wooden door and opened it slightly. "M. Cooper is here, sir"

A pleasant baritone voice said, "Send him in."

The woman walked up to Margaret and said, "I thought you were a man. Get out now." She walked past Margaret and sat at the desk.

Margaret felt insulted. How dare anyone, let alone another woman, tell her she was not good enough. She glared at the woman as she walked through the door.

Inside, Mr. Ross studied Margaret for a moment. He was a tall, handsome man in his forties with a clean shaven face and flecks of white at his temples. He smiled. "I'm so glad to see you. Please, come in and sit down." He indicated a sofa with a table in front of it.

Margaret said, "Thank you for seeing me Mr. Ross."

"Please call me Harold."

"Thank you. I'm Margaret. "

Ross sat down next to her. "Now, let's have a look at your portfolio." He moved close in as she flipped through the pages. He praised every drawing, pointing out how the hatch marks created depth and complemented her superb command of form. Margaret swelled with pride over the compliments. Here was someone who could help make her career.

"You know, Margaret, publishing is a small community. We know each other, and though we compete, we are all friendly. You have to be friendly to get by in this business, especially if you're a woman."

"Oh, I can be friendly, Harold. I grew up in a small farming community. Everyone's friendly."

"Indeed. Would you like some wine?"

"I… don't really drink, Harold, except for a sip at communion."

"Everyone in the business does. It's just friendly."

"Well, in that case, just a little."

Ross got up and poured two large glasses of wine from a bottle on a credenza. He returned, handed one to Margaret and sat even closer to her. She took a sip and coughed, then smiled sheepishly. Ross said, "There, that's much friendlier. Go ahead, take a good drink."

They sat and drank and talked about her illustrations. Ross poured her another glass of wine. Margaret felt slightly light headed. She found herself smiling and began to giggle.

Ross put his half-finished glass down. "See. It's fun being friendly." Slowly his hand moved to her knee. Margaret didn't take notice at first. She finished the second glass of wine and felt very relaxed. His hand moved up toward her thigh. "Harold. I don't feel so good. I think I'll go home."

"Just lay back on the sofa."

She felt too woozy to do much else. He pushed here down and kissed her hard. Then, he thrust his hand under her skirt and up her leg. Margaret pushed back. "No. Stop."

"We're going to get real friendly little farm girl." Ross tossed off his suit jacket and undid the fly of his trousers. Margaret fought as he reached under her skirt and ripped her bloomers off. All the haze of the wine evaporated in her head. She held her legs tightly together. Ross sneered as he laughed. His head was on her belly and his arms were wrapped around her back. Margaret slapped him across the cheek, "Leave me alone. Get off me."

He sneered even broader. "So, you like to play rough. I can play rough." He slapped her back and pulled up her skirt as he raised his body and inched up on her.

Margaret snapped her right knee up in a jerk and jammed it into his crotch. Ross cried out and rolled onto the floor. Margaret ran to the door and found it locked. The editor was getting to his feet. "You little bitch. You'll pay."

There was an open window to her left with a fire escape just outside. Bounding across the floor, she climbed through the window and down the fire escape as quickly as possible.

She ran panting and shaking as fast as she could away from the building in her disheveled clothes, certain everyone was staring at her. Then, she slowed and roamed down several streets in no particular direction. She spotted a police station. Inside, the desk sergeant was reading a newspaper. He looked down at Margaret. "Yes?"

"Please. Help. I've just been attacked. Someone tried to compromise my virtue."

"What's your name?"

"Margaret Cooper."

"Where do you live."

"I'm staying in a boarding house, but I just moved from a small town in New Jersey."

"I see. Were there any witnesses?"

"No. We were alone behind a locked door."

"Without a witness it's your word against his. There's nothing I can do."

"But this is a powerful man preying on young women. Harold Ross."

"The editor? Take my advice. You don't want to mess with him. Just forget it."

"But he'll do it again. He made me drink wine?"

"Made or offered?"

"He said it was normal."

"Sure. For all I know you're a gold digger trying to get at his money and he spurned you. You wouldn't be the first. Look, it's late, I don't want any extra paperwork, especially over a country floozy. Just go back to your small town and forget this ever happened."

Margaret sat on her bed that night and cried as she never had before. She felt filthy in a way that no amount of dirt could make her. There was an unsettling hollowness in her chest as though she was caving in on herself. Was it her fault? Had she encouraged him? Did she misunderstand his intentions? "No," she said aloud in the room as she realized that the woman in the office had been warning her. Perhaps she wasn't cut out for life in a big city. Perhaps she should just go back to the farm and forget her dreams. What kind of fool was she?

The tears stopped. She stood up and gave a roaring shout out a window to all of New York. "I did nothing wrong and I am not going back. If I have to be tough I will be tougher than you. I will become an illustrator in this city and men will respect me. Everyone will respect me!"

She took out her master drawings and re-created her portfolio.

Four days later she had an appointment with another editor. She held her head high as she walked into the reception area fifteen minutes early. A male clerk looked up from his desk. "May I help you?"

"I'm M. Cooper. I have an appointment with Mr. Wilkins."

The clerk stared at her for a moment. "You're M. Cooper? Really." A wry smile formed on his lips. "Won't you come this way?" He led her to an oak door and opened it. "Mr. Wilkins. M. Cooper is here." He ushered Margaret in.

The office was large but stuffed with filing cabinets, shelves and papers. There was no couch, only chairs. She checked for the windows.

Wilkins was looking down at his desk as he went through some papers. "Please come in, I was just examining your portfolio and …" He looked up with a perplexed look on his face. "Jenkins, where's Mr. Cooper?"

"This is Miss Cooper, sir. Miss M. Cooper."

Margaret stepped forward. "Actually, it's Margaret Cooper, Mr. Wilkins. Thank you for offering me a chance to show my work."

"I see. Your…your work is very fine, which is why I sent for you. At this moment I don't have an assignment, but I will keep your work on file and notify you if something comes up. Do we have Miss Cooper's address, Mr. Jenkins?"

"Yes, sir."

Margaret said, "Mr. Wilkins, thank you for the kind words, but please tell me honestly. Is the lack of assignments because I am a woman?"

"Not at all. The moment something comes up, I will contact you."

"Mr. Wilkins, if I were to bring you something unique, something no one else had drawn, would you publish it?"

"Of course. We are always looking for a scoop. If you come across something bring it right in. You can make certain Miss Cooper gets to see me right away, Jenkins."

Jenkins still held his half smile. "Of course, sir."

Whenever Margaret went out she took a sketch pad and pencil. A horse bolted and carried its carriage and driver careening through the streets, but there were already two men with sketch pads drawing feverishly. Every time she came upon an interesting subject another artist was there, always a man.

She never gave up. Every day she was on the streets or going through the parks in search of a unique subject that no one else had captured. Summer was waning into fall when she heard people shouting. She followed the noise to find the top floor of a three-story stone building in flames. The flames lapped out of tall windows to lick at the intricate architectural detail of the building. Along the top of the roof, a young girl, no more than four, was trapped by the fire. She cried and looked over the edge. The fire brigade had arrived but their ladders could not reach the child.

The blaze shot out of nearly every window of the top floor. A fireman climbed up a ladder as far as he could, then started scaling the stone outcrops of the outside wall. Margaret began sketching quickly, catching impressions of the unfolding scene as she ran forward.

The fire brigade unfolded a safety net and eight men held onto its edges. The fireman reached one of the windows that was not yet burning. Flames shot out of it and he pulled himself up by the keystone in the window's arch. Margaret caught every move in crude strokes.

The fireman reached the roof and swept the child up in his arms. He stood at the edge and rocked back and forth before jumping. People below gasped. Some fainted. The fireman landed on his back into the safety net, the little girl held to his chest.

Cheers erupted. Margaret was close enough to see the fireman's face and see the girl crying. She ran around a corner and hailed a cab, instructing the driver to reach Mr. Wilkins's office as quickly as possible. She selected three of the drawings and worked to clean them up before the cab arrived.

She rushed into the reception area. "Mr. Jenkins, I must see Mr. Williams at once. I have a scoop."

Jenkins knocked on Mr. Wilkin's door. "Sir. Miss Cooper has returned with a scoop."

Wilkin's looked at the three illustrations. "He crawled up the building? Amazing. You say there were no other reporters there?"

"I looked and saw no one."

"Jenkins. Get a reporter up here to take Miss Cooper's story."

"Then you're going to print my illustrations?"

"Young lady, this is pure journalism. You're hired."

Margaret floated back into the reception area.

Jenkins's half smile was a full grin. "Welcome aboard."

"Thank you."

"You know, he's paying you less than the men."

"Yes. I know. But this is a victory. I'm published."

She took a week before returning home for the rest of her things.

She had sent a telegram to her mother with the good news about her new job. She knew her grandmother would be thrilled. Margaret would pay her back all the money once she got a paycheck.

She reached the station. Her mother and father were waiting. Margaret ran up and hugged them both. "Where's Grammy?"

Her father took her hand. "Sweetie, your grandmother passed away in her sleep last night while you were traveling. It was sudden. No one expected it. She read your telegram and was so proud of you."

Her mother had a smirk on her face. "It was old age, Margaret. Nothing we could do. It was just her time."

"Prudence. If you couldn't respect your mother in life, at least have some respect for the dead."

The trip back to the farm was the longest Margaret had ever known. Her grandmother lay in a coffin in the parlor. Mourners came all day. They brought hams and pies and cakes and bread. People recited the events of her long life and many tears were shed. Margaret sat, dazed, as she received condolences from the guests.

The funeral was held in the church cemetery the next day. The pastor read a eulogy. Margaret sat with her brothers and remained stoic though she wanted nothing more than to run to the ocean. Everyone greeted Margaret and her family as they left the church.

At home, Margaret began going through her things and deciding what she wanted to take to New York. She went into the hall and knocked on her grandmother's door out of habit before realizing there would be no answer. She pushed the door open and peered inside. Everything was as she remembered it, except for the dresser top. All the shells were missing. She went downstairs and found her mother.

"Where are Grammy's seashells?"

"I threw them back in the ocean."

"Why? I wanted to take some as a memento."

"Because we need to clear that nonsense from this house. Look what it did to you. Running off to New York."

"I have a job there. Aren't you proud of that?"

"Pride before the fall. Do you think those men will allow you to really succeed? They'll use you and toss you aside. This is the kind of absurdity your grandmother sowed in your head. Well, the world isn't a magical place where you just wish for something. Those shells are best where they are and you'll do best to forget them, too. "

"Why did you always hate Grammy?"

"Don't be impertinent, child. She doted on you. I should have taken a firmer hand. It's all over, Margaret. Grow up."

"What made you so bitter? You've always fought everything I wanted."

"Because you wanted the fantasy world. Don't you think that I have your best interest at heart? Have always had it at heart? Every mother wants her daughter to be happy. But you can't be happy if you ignore the real world. It will smother you otherwise."

"What is the choice I face, mother?"

"Live in reality or lose everything."

"That's not what Grammy meant. Before I left she told me it was coming. You know what it is and it scares you."

Her mother left the room without another word.

Margaret walked down to the beach. The sand was warm in the sun. She stood there for a long time and didn't think of anything in particular as she listened to the waves. Their tuneless music sounded sweet and sorrowful at the same time. An urge welled up to strip off her clothes and dive into them to swim forever.

She looked down. A small, broken shell lay half buried in the sand. She reached down and dusted it off. It had been an oyster once, a living thing, now shattered and dead. She held it in her hand and studied its craggy surface whose ridges resembled mountain ranges.

The shell returned to New York with her. She kept it when she and John were married. It traveled the world with her, until it slipped out of her hand while they were on a ship bound for Java and fell overboard. John had held her close as she cried that night for the memory of her grandmother.

As she stood on the rocky beach next to Ian's dock, the memory faded to the back of her mind. She absently scanned the shore as though she might see the shell wash up mysteriously. It was the kind of thing her grandmother would tell her and she smiled.

She returned from the dock and saw Sara standing at the outside well, completely naked. The young woman repeatedly lowered a bucket, drew up water, and poured it over her head. Margaret watched, transfixed, as the water flowed down her shoulders, over her slim body, and onto the muddy ground. The sun glistened on her skin, making the drops of water seem like jewels.

Sara either didn't see Margaret or she took no notice of her as she softly sang a strange song to herself. The words were nonsense, yet Margaret found the melody hauntingly familiar. It conjured images of swimming free through rolling waves in the ocean. Margaret closed her eyes and imagined cool, crisp water flowing past her and the rush of the ocean's surge as kelp beds waved in the current. Out of the babble, words slowly emerged.

> *Dive deep,*
> *Beneath the ocean waves,*
> *The water rushing by;*
>
> *Embrace the everlasting thrill,*
> *For we shall never die.*

Margaret swayed in the morning sun as she began to sing along with Sara. The words came easily, as though she had known them all her life. After a while, she realized that she was singing alone. She opened her eyes to find Sara staring at her. It seemed odd to Margaret that the young woman showed no sense of shame at her nakedness, nor did she make an attempt to cover herself.

Sara said, "I thought you went to the village today."

Margaret's hands shook as she was pulled back from the image of the sea. "Mr. Talbot went. I've stayed to work on some drawings."

Sara clapped and hopped in the mud. "Oh, that's fantastic. You can come and pick berries with me. They're ever so sweet. I'd never tasted anything like them until Ian brought me here."

Margaret tried not to stare at Sara's nude form. "I'm sure you had sweet things where you come from."

"Not like berries." Sara bound forward and took Margaret's hand. "Come on. Let's go." Then, an uncommonly serious look filled the young woman's face. "You won't tell Ian about this, will you?"

"About being outside without clothes?"

Sara laughed again. "Oh, he doesn't care about that. He's seen me naked plenty of times. He likes it." She giggled before turning serious once more. "I meant the bucket."

"Bucket?"

"Yes. When he finds me pouring water over myself it disturbs him."

Margaret helped Sara select some appropriate clothes for berry picking, but informed her that she could not go along. "I have work to do, and Thomas Brown is coming over at noon for an art lesson. I was hoping you might stay long enough to see him."

Sara adjusted a wide-brimmed hat. "Thomas is so sweet, but so sad. He draws pictures of birds and trees for me." She pulled on leather gloves. "I wish I could stay, but I have to gather berries. I promised Ian a treat tonight."

Margaret began to worry about Thomas's visit and the power of gossip. "Do you know a woman named Beth Ramsey?"

"Oh yes. She thinks I'm a witch. When I first came she used to hide in the forest and watch me all the time. I asked her to have tea but she never came in, so I stopped asking. Once in a while I still see her across the road. It seems like a silly game, but she likes it, so I let her play."

"When was the last time you saw her?"

Sara took off the gloves and tried another pair. "June. She sat out there all morning."

Margaret wished the Grants had a telephone so she could warn Thomas. All she could do was prepare for his lesson and hope Beth Ramsey didn't see them together.

"Sara, I'd like to get into the carriage house. Can you open it for me?"

Sara said, "No one goes in the carriage house. It's where Ian keeps his yesterday."

"His what?"

"His yesterday. Too much of it is sad. He used to be there all the time, because that's where Lizzie and Samuel are. He'd talk to them there and sit in the carriage and remember. But, he knew he had to release the yesterday to live with me. So he locked the carriage house."

Margaret didn't understand what Sara was saying but saw the young woman would be no help to her. She could abandon the carriage house and look for another place, but it was so perfect. Whatever she did, it had to be fast.

Sara left to gather berries and Margaret went out back to inspect the lock on the carriage house. It was sturdy. Without a key, she stood little chance of entry. The sun was rising overhead and already, the morning was turning warm. She checked the nurse's watch. Thomas would arrive in two hours.

Once more, Margaret tried to think of a place to paint. Nothing fit like the carriage house. She walked around the building and inspected the windows to see if one was loose. None would open. She came to the building's east side that faced away from both the house and the road.

The windows were of uniform size, except for one in the northeast corner that was notably narrower. Upon closer examination, a faint line that was obscured by many layers of paint could be made out above and to either side of it.

She ran inside the house and got the poker from the fireplace and a sharp knife from the kitchen. Carefully, she scored the paint along the line, jammed the poker into it and pried. A door that had been nailed shut and painted over popped partially out from the exterior wall. She stepped back, ran forward and pushed with all her weight. The door swung inward with a cracking sound.

The light in the carriage house was surprisingly bright, though the air was permeated with the dry smell of dust. Boxes and trunks were stacked neatly on shelves. A few trunks were strewn across the floor. She inspected the carriage. Its seats were tooled of fine leather and the lamps were trimmed with gold. The driver's bench sat high, facing forward. Behind it were twin seats facing each other and protected at ground level by black, lacquered doors.

Margaret had ridden in such carriages and wondered how Ian had come to possess it and what it was doing there. Anna might be able to tell, but Margaret was reluctant to draw attention to her interest in the carriage house.

As she looked for a suitable place to set up an easel, her eye strayed to the dust on the floor. There were footprints, and the marks of something having been recently dragged across it. She followed the marks to an open steamer trunk at the rear of the carriage.

Inside she found a top hat, a woman's corset, a frock coat, some ties, and a pair of button shoes. They looked to be about thirty years out of fashion. At the bottom of the chest were photographs. There was a tall woman with dark hair whose smile was blurred by the long exposure of the picture. Next to her was a man in a merchant captain's uniform who was clearly a younger Ian. Behind them was a three-masted sailing vessel.

Other photos lay in the trunk. Margaret recognized many scenes from her own travels around the world. In every picture where he appeared, Ian smiled a bright grin. The unnamed woman smiled too. Hers was quiet, content, yet filled with no less joy then Ian's. In one picture the woman held an infant in her arms, her smile the broadest of all in that photograph.

The woman had to be Lizzie and the infant Samuel. The time and costumes fit. It was also apparent that Ian had been a sea captain. This explained how he had earned enough money to buy the carriage.

She carefully put everything back and resumed her search for a suitable place to set up her easel. Thomas would be there soon and she wanted to be ready.

A crude staircase at the back of the building led to a loft. No one looking in from ground level would be able to see her up there, and a round window in the gable end of the carriage house provided plenty of light.

Pleased, she returned to the house and removed Blossom's portrait from the trunk. It took three trips to transport it and the supplies to the loft. With the easel set up, she placed Blossom's portrait on it and felt at ease for the first time since arriving at the Grants' home.

She worked out a plan in her head. Even if Sara was in the house, she would not be able to see anyone entering the door that had been blocked up. Margaret would simply say that she was going for a walk to refresh her artistic Muse. People wanted to believe that artists needed to draw strength from the elements of nature or some other mysterious place. She considered the whole notion to be completely absurd, but she played along when it suited her wants.

She set out some brushes and tubes of paint, then assembled a second collapsible easel and placed the blank canvas it. After inspecting everything, she started down the steps, then stopped. For reasons she could not explain, she covered the portrait of Blossom and placed it in a corner.

Margaret snapped off the tapered end of an old paintbrush and wedged it between the bottom of the door and the wall before returning to the house. Soon after, a timid knock came. Thomas stood at the threshold, twisting his cap in his hands. She beckoned him in. "I'm so pleased you've come."

He scuffed the floor with his feet. "I'm sorry abou' making a fool of myself yesterday. I've thought a lot since then. What with my dad drowning before I was born and the other boys always teasing me about the seizures, I've had to be pretty tough growing up. I guess I got a little too tough. I can't always see when someone wants to be a friend." He looked up at her. "Please take me as a student. I don't have much money but I'll pay you what I can. I promise I won't be tough with you again."

Margaret felt deeply moved by the vulnerability he displayed. "I don't want any money from you. I just want to help you find the talent you have inside. As for being tough, we'll forget the past and start fresh today with your first lesson. But, before we begin I have a secret that you must promise to keep."

He formed his brow into a serious frown. "What secret?"

 "Follow me."

She led him around to the door of the carriage house and opened it.

Thomas inspected the opening carefully. "I didn't know this was here."

"That is part of the secret you must keep. No one can know that I've pried this door open or that we've been inside. Understand?"

"Ian will be very angry if he finds out."

"I know that, Thomas, but it's the only place I can safely set up my easel to work and teach. Are you willing to keep the secret?"

He looked around as though expecting Ian to walk in at any time. "I will not betray you."

She smiled. "Good."

When they climbed to the loft, she said, "I want to teach you about painting."

"I thought you were going to teach me to draw better. It's all I've ever done."

"Your drawings are masterful. I can teach you very little that you don't already know. What I can teach you is how to paint."

"That's just drawing with a brush."

Margaret set out a clean palette along with some tubes of paint and three brushes. "Is that what you think?"

"Isn't it?"

"There are quite a few differences, as you'll see in a moment. First of all, a brush is not a pencil and canvas is not paper. These, however, are the mechanical craft elements. You need something else to create art."

She stood in front of him. "If I wanted to paint a picture of your hand, what would I need to do first?"

Thomas thought for a moment. "Mix the paint?"

"I would have to do that, yes, but not first."

He shook his head. "I don't know."

"Look at the palm of your hands, Thomas. What do you see?"

"Fingers. A wrist."

"That's what an ordinary person sees. An artist sees beyond the physical. When I look at your hands I see calluses. From them I see back to all the boats you've scraped and repaired and painted over the years that gave you the calluses. I see hard work and sweat. I see devotion for your job. And because of that I see a stalwart, reliable heart that the people of Glasen can count on every day of every year. That is what an artist sees."

Thomas turned his hands over. "All that from these?"

"You have to look below the surface. To create art, you start with something in the real world. From that, you draw an idea, like a hardworking young man who can be trusted. You keep this idea in the back of your mind as you work, and when you finally see your idea expressed on the canvas, the painting is completed. You've already done this without realizing it. Think of your drawing of Sara and Ian. You captured the emotions they felt, not just their bodies. Look at the world around you, this minute, and pull an idea from it, the most important idea you can think of."

Thomas blushed bright red. "I'm not certain."

"Come now, Thomas. No one who blushes like that is uncertain. You're an artist. You have to push aside concerns about what's polite or acceptable. You can't worry about what your mother will say. What are you thinking right now?"

He looked down at the wide floorboards. "I was thinking abou' a portrait of you. I want to show how smart and beautiful you are."

The innocence of his answer surprised her, and at the same time, filled her with delight. "I'm flattered."

"Would you sit for me, Mrs. Talbot?"

The question was asked as though the young man would wilt were she to reject him. She reached out and gently touched his arm. "It would be an honor to sit for you. I won't be able to watch as you work, but maybe that's better. The canvas is set up on the easel. There are the charcoals. Begin with a rough sketch directly on the canvas. It doesn't have to be exact or detailed. The sketch will only serve as a guide." She pulled a trunk out from next to the wall and sat down. "Is this all right?"

"I've never made a picture straight from a person. Every picture I've ever done was drawn under my tree."

"Just paint what you see with your eyes instead of what you remember. You do that very well in your drawings. Try to look past the physical and feel how the subject impresses you. Seek out the thoughts you have and the emotions you feel. Don't be afraid to do something outlandish to express them."

She instructed him in the method Robert Henri had taught her. Thomas struggled with mixing paints, but soon learned how to find the color he wanted. He painted, looked at his work, scraped pain off and tried again. He shook his head and sighed from time to time. Margaret repeated a lecture from her own training. She stopped him several times to inspect his progress and make corrections.

His frustration grew until he stepped back from the easel and flung his brush to the floor. "I'll never do this. The paint won't go on correctly. I want to show the sparkle in your eyes and everything's flat. This is the hardest thing I've ever done." He sat down on a trunk with his head in his hands.

Margaret sat down next to him and placed her arms around his shoulders. "So, painting is hard. If you've learned nothing else today, you've still had the most successful lesson in your artistic life."

After Thomas left, Margaret cleaned up and returned to the house. She spread her sketches of Glasen across the dining room table. For two hours she worked at turning the rough images into full drawings ready for the engraver. Sara came in with a basket of berries in each hand. "Oh, Margaret. I wish you had come with me. The berries stretched on for miles. We could have picked enough to have pies every day for a month." She placed the baskets on the kitchen table. "We must get ready for supper. Ian just unloaded his catch at the wharf and is rowing back home."

Margaret smiled. "Did a little bird tell you?"

Sara looked at her with a puzzled look. "Why would a bird tell me that?"

"It's just a saying."

"Oh. Well, anyway, it was a wave."

A few minutes later, Margaret heard the sound of a surrey. The front door opened and John walked in. A moment later Anna and Alistair Lamont came through the door. Alistair removed his hat. "Good evening, Mrs. Talbot. I trust you're well."

"Yes, thank you."

Anna said, "Is Sara home?"

"She's in the kitchen."

"Sara," said Anna loudly, "We've brought a surprise."

Sara came in from the kitchen as an elderly man wearing an immaculate suit and gloves entered the house. Under his right arm he carried a porcelain cremation urn.

Sara jumped up and down and clapped her hands together as she made a squeal. "Mr. Sinclair." She put her hands on the urn. "And Mary. You both look so wonderful this evening."

Sinclair said, "Thank you."

Sara took the man's free hand and led him over to Margaret. "Obviously you've met Mr. Talbot. Allow me to introduce his wife, the very famous Margaret Talbot. Margaret Talbot, may I introduce Angus and Mary Sinclair."

Margaret stared at the urn. "How do you do?"

"Quite fine, thank you," said Sinclair. "We were just over visiting Anna and Alistair when Mr. Talbot arrived, so we asked if we could come along as we haven't been out this way in ages, have we, Mary?" He looked down at the urn.

Ian came in from the kitchen. "Anna. Alistair." He then noticed Sinclair and smiled. "Angus. Mary. I'm so glad to see you. It's been too long." He shook Sinclair's hand firmly. "Are those new gloves you're wearing?"

"Aye. Just in from Eaton's."

Ian leaned over and spoke to the urn. "You'd better be careful, Mary. He's getting too handsome for his own good. The woman will be throwing' themselves at him.'"

Sinclair laughed. "Oh, pshaw. I've got all the girl I can handle, and the prettiest one at that." He patted the urn softly.

Sara went off to the kitchen. Everyone else went into the living room. Ian told stories about fishing. Sinclair followed each word with rapt attention as Alistair fingered his watch fob and John made notes. Margaret followed the conversation, but felt she could not ask the one question she really wanted of Angus Sinclair.

"And so," Ian said as he concluded a story, "I pulled in the line and kelp was wound around every hook. I had to pick it out of each one because the weight would have sunk the dory. I thought I'd never get home."

"Why didn't you cut the line?" said John.

Ian's eyes widened. "And lose all those hooks?"

Everyone laughed.

Sinclair leaned over to Ian. "I have to take a little walk outside." He sat the urn down on the couch next to Anna. "If you'll take care of my dear Mary, I'll be right back."

Ian stood up. "I need to speak with Sara, if you'll excuse me."

Margaret stared at the urn and looked up at Anna. "Is it really his wife in there?"

Anna stroked the urn. "Angus and Mary were married just shy of a year when they came to the gold fields. He was one of the more successful miners. Seemed to have a knack for finding just the place to stake a claim.

"He was working a shallow tunnel with a rich vein. Their cabin was close by and every day she brought him his lunch. They were very sweet and Alistair would make special runs to bring their supplies.

"One day the tunnel started to crumble. Angus had gone up for some timbers to shore it up just as Mary arrived with his lunch. He just saw her go down in the mine seconds before the whole thing collapsed.

"His picks and shovels were inside the tunnel, so he dug with his bare hands, calling her name as he went. Two other miners heard his cry and came to help, but when they reached her, she was dead. Old Tom

McPherson said Angus just held Mary in his arms and wept like a baby. Her head had been smashed in so that Tom said you couldn't recognize her." Anna reached over and put her hand on the urn. "I guess that's why Angus had her remains cremated. To purify the disfigurement."

Alistair nodded. "He was never right after that. I'm sure he blamed himself. It was the end of his prospecting days, but he'd taken in enough gold to live on for the rest of his life. He bought a house in the village and placed the urn on the mantel in the parlor. When we went to visit he sometimes got up and talked to it, saying how much he missed his sweet Mary and how lonely he felt. After a while, the urn vanished from the mantel. When I asked him where it was, he said he had put it on the chest of drawers in his bedroom. Soon after that it moved to the little table next to his bed.

"One morning, I went over to visit when he was recovering from an illness. There was no answer at the door, so I went inside, worried he had fallen ill again. I found him asleep in bed with his arms wrapped around the urn."

Anna said, "Now he takes it with him everywhere he goes. He talks to it and listens to it as though it were Mary come back to life, or, in his view, never having left. Everyone in Glasen talks to it and listens to it just the same as he does."

Margaret shook her head. "You don't believe this is Mary Sinclair, do you?"

Anna said, "Now, who's to say if it is or if it isn't? Angus believes it is. In his mind Mary is sitting right here on the couch, as pretty as she ever was."

"But, it's a delusion, a dream world. Someone needs to make him wake up and see reality."

"Dreams are very powerful, Margaret. Think abou' the ones you've let go of and allowed to fade. Any one of them could have happened. But were they any less real when they were your dreams?"

Margaret now heard her own mother's voice in the words she had just spoken and felt a sick pit in her stomach. She looked across the room to where John sat uncomfortably with his notebook open before him.

Supper was both exotic and exquisite. Sara prepared squash and berries, a combination that Margaret was certain would be repulsive but that tasted wonderful. Pan-fried haddock, in a delicious sauce Margaret could not identify, made up the main course. Various vegetables and herbs complemented it.

Ian had brought in a board to extend the table and a plate was set at every place, including that of the funeral urn. As they ate, Sinclair told stories from his mining days.

Anna got up from her chair. "Well, it's late and we all have things to do in the morning."

Sinclair picked up the urn. "Quite right. Mary and I have chores, and Ian has fishing. It's been nice to meet you, Mr. And Mrs. Talbot. I hope we can visit again."

"We'll be staying a few more weeks," said Margaret.

Sinclair gave a wide smile. "That means we'll see each other at the ceilidh."

"Ceilidh?"

"Yes. To celebrate the fall colors."

Anna, Alistair and Sinclair rode off into the night. Margaret thought about the fuss made over the urn, and wondered if any of her friends would ever go to such lengths on her behalf. Would John?

CHAPTER SEVEN

The days slowly turned from hot and humid to warm and pleasant. The nights were sometimes cool, and Ian often lit a fire in the parlor hearth. John continued to ride into the village with Anna every morning. Margaret sometimes accompanied him to make new sketches, but spent much of her time at the Grants' house to refine the rough drawings. It was tedious work that required time and concentration. Form and dimensions had to be suggested with lines and hatch marks. There were none of the subtleties of oil painting.

Thomas continued to come to the loft secretly for lessons. He made steady progress on the portrait of Margaret as his control of paint and brush advanced. Each time he visited, she covered the portrait of Blossom and set it in a corner.

One morning, Margaret misplaced a drawing of the church's altar. It would be a simple matter to draw it again, but she had liked the treatment of the subject and wanted to find the original.

While searching in the bedroom, she spied a piece of drawing paper stuffed between the wooden bedpost and the wall. She smoothed it open across the bed.

It was not one of her drawings. The paper contained words penned in John's bold handwriting. As she looked closer, she realized it was not a note at all.

I watch
Unseen
Protecting one I cannot touch
A flower locked away in glass
More precious than my breath
My heart beats hollow
She stands
Arm's length away
A living ghost
Veiled in shadow

Each sight of her
Bores through my chest
To crack the soul encased

I taste each breath she draws
Unable to respond
Chained by duty
Oceans of duty
Oceans to drown the meaning of duty
One touch upon her cheek
~~Would lead to~~
~~Would become~~
~~Would have a~~
~~Would be to~~

At the bottom of the page the words, "*God help me*" were raggedly scrawled.

Margaret had never known John to write poetry. She stared at the paper as she tried to make sense of what he meant by duty. Rage built within her as she thought of how he had callously abandoned his duty to her after the baby's death. Yet there was grief in the poem, mixed with remorse. Clearly, he felt something intense in spite of the exterior he projected.

Her first reaction was to confront John and force him to explain himself. She read the poem several more times. "Why can't you say this to me?" she shouted to the empty room.

In the end, she crumpled the paper up the way she had found it and stuffed it back behind the bedpost.

When John and Anna returned from the village that evening, Anna said, "Mrs. Gunn wanted to know if you would be available for tea on Friday afternoon. She wants to ask a few ladies to come over and hear of your adventures. I think she'd like to see some of your drawings, too. I hope it's not a bother."

"I'd be happy to, Anna. I'll bring a few sketches I've been working on. Why don't I just ride in with you and John and save you a trip?"

On Thursday morning, Margaret sat at the dining room table and touched up a portrait of Phillip Lamont that she wanted to present at tea the next day. She smiled to herself, remembering the pride he'd shown while standing in his parlor with the boys fidgeting next to him. Phillip's half-hearted threats for them to stand still had had no effect, but when Anna arrived and said she was going to make some fruit fingers and that all good little boys could have some, the brothers had become instantly attentive.

Margaret worried in the details of Phillip's parlor with its flower wallpaper, rosette door moldings, and glass beads on the shades of the oil lamps. It was a purely mechanical exercise. Would anyone appreciate the lives of the people the drawing represented? The magazine containing the future article would likely be tossed out, or perhaps used to line a bird cage, once it was read.

Would Blossom's portrait meet with such a shallow reception? Or would the observers look past the obvious to see a strength of character that had conquered slavery? That was certainly Margaret's intention, but the harder she toiled, the further she seemed to be from her goal. It had been days since she had last worked on it.

She felt a sudden contempt for the sketch in front of her. Three hours of her life wasted on a drawing that might be rejected by her editor, three hours in which she could have been painting.

When she'd first started illustrating, she was excited. It was heady to be honored at parties and accept awards. There was a drunken excitement to those days. Now, the urgency to paint grew incessantly within her. She stared at the illustration on the table and tried to find some meaning in it. Nothing came to her.

Sara entered from the kitchen with a platter of smoked fish. "Are you hungry? It's past noon."

As Margaret smelled the herb-laden aroma she realized that she *was* hungry. Sara set out two plates along with some berries, a block of cheese, and tea, which she served at every meal and occasion.

After lunch, Margaret wiped her mouth with a linen napkin. "That was amazing, Sara. I wish I could cook as well as you. Perhaps you can write down some of your recipes for me."

Sara looked at her quizzically. "Write down what?"

"You know. Recipes."

"What does that mean?"

"Recipes are written instructions for preparing particular kinds of food."

Sara continued to stare at her. "Why would you want that?"

"So you can cook the same thing again."

Sara's puzzled look deepened. "Do people cook the same thing twice?"

At first it seemed that Sara was playing at not understanding, but then Margaret realized that the young woman was truly confused by the idea. "Sara. Doesn't Ian have some special thing he likes you to make?"

"I don't know. He's never said. When he comes home from the sea I listen to how he feels, and I cook what he needs."

Sara seemed to think this an adequate explanation, but it left Margaret puzzled. "We can talk about this later. I need to take a walk right now. I'll be back in a few hours."

"Are you searching for your Muse again?"

"Yes. That's right." Margaret felt a twist of guilt at lying to Sara, but knew she had no alternative if she was going to continue using the carriage house to paint.

When she climbed up to the loft, she discovered she had left her painting uncovered the last time she had been up there. It felt strange to find Blossom's image sitting out on the easel when it had spent so many months hiding in the rear of a trunk. A giddy thrill ran through her at the site of the painting displayed openly. An instant later, she remembered that her studio was only a storage loft in a forbidden carriage house. "Is that what freedom is, Blossom? Something you can dream about but never wake up to?"

She mixed some colors and began work on one arm, scraped the paint off, and reworked it. This cycle was repeated a dozen times before she sat the brush down to study the canvas. Blossom's arms still appeared limp and ineffectual. The eyes failed to show the determination Margaret strove for.

A sense of doubt tinged with anger pulled on her. "Blossom. Am I really an artist?"

The sound of footsteps came from the bottom of the wooden stairs. *Ian*. What would she say? Could she crawl through the window in the gable end of the wall unnoticed?

Thomas's voice rose up the stairs in a whisper. "Mrs. Talbot? Are you there?"

Margaret noticed just how hard her heart was pounding. "Did anyone see you come in?"

"No. Sara's inside baking. When she said you had gone for a walk I knew where you had to be, but I just told her that I'd come back later."

Guiltily, she realized that Thomas was now entwined in her lie as well. "Is the door closed downstairs?"

"Yes," he said as he appeared at the top of the stairs. His shoes were polished and his hair neatly combed. He held a leather satchel in one hand.

He walked steadily toward her until he was inches away. He reached out and touched her cheek. "You've been crying."

She felt her face flush. "It's sometimes part of the creative process."

Thomas turned and looked at the painting of Blossom, inspecting it with wide eyes. "Magnificent."

Margaret wished she had covered the portrait. "I have a long way to go yet. It doesn't quite express that certain thing."

"Oh, but it does. Look at her eyes. Look at what she's saying. She's been beaten, hurt, used up. All she has left is resignation. Nothing worse can happen to her, but nothing better can either."

Margaret shook her head. "That's not what it says. The eyes show fortitude and determination where the arms signify her deep strength."

"There's no strength left in her, Mrs. Talbot. She's all used up and no one's ever going to give her anymore." He turned slowly to her. "It's a self-portrait, isn't it?"

She forced a laugh. "No. She's a woman I met in Alabama."

Again, he softly stroked her cheek. "I see it in your eyes."

She wanted to step back and tell him to stop touching her, but she said nothing. His stare left her feeling more exposed than if she had stood naked before him. She wanted Thomas to leave her alone so she could think, and yet she wanted him to stay near.

He walked across the loft and stared out the oval window. "You're as hard as nails on the outside. It's inside where you're caving in on yourself." He turned around and faced her. "You've given up on having what you want."

Though she tried to sound confident, her voice cracked. "How could you know what I want?"

"You said it yourself abou' me. I see things in people. I always have. That's why I can draw, I guess. I know what people are thinking and I put that on the paper." He reached into the satchel and handed her a drawing. "I made this yesterday. That's why I came over, to show it to you."

Instead of quickly scanning the drawing, she studied it slowly, seeing the picture rather than the lines. She was the subject, wearing a classical Greek dress made of sheer material with the right breast exposed. She stood on the ridge of a hill, her feet pointing to one side and her head turned to the other. Her eyes were sad, filled with disappointment and regret, a woman caught between two worlds, unable to step into either.

"It's how you are right now," said Thomas, "Powerful but exhausted. There's no one to breathe life into you anymore, just people who want to take it."

"Thomas, you can't draw things like this, it's too personal. I can't teach you if you..." She looked into his eyes. Then they were in each other's arms, holding tightly, stroking, kissing. Passions she thought long dead surged through her. He kissed her lips, her forehead, her neck. She wrapped her arms around him as her knees went weak.

She pushed herself back, shaking as she breathed raggedly. "Oh God. Oh dear God. What have I done? You have to go, Thomas. You can't stay."

"I love you, Margaret."

"Don't say that. I'm a married woman. I'm your teacher."

"He doesn't care abou' you."

She covered her ears with her hands. "It doesn't matter."

"I love you, Margaret. I want to sing your praises. I want to make your dreams come true. Let me give you back the life he's taken from you. You're more than a good artist, you're great."

She felt paralyzed. "It's wrong. Don't you understand?"

"You need to be loved." He reached out. "Take my hand."

"Thomas, don't."

"Take it. Please."

She told herself to run, but found herself reaching out and putting her hand in his. She drew him closer, looked into his eyes, and reached out with her other hand to touch his face. As she did, his eyes started to roll up into his lids. His body convulsed as gurgled rasps came from his mouth.

In panic, she looked around for help, knowing there was none. She quickly lowered Thomas to the floor. His body jerked with a seizure. Margaret sat on the floor and placed his head in her lap so he wouldn't bang it against the boards. She felt desperately helpless and wondered if that was what John felt when she lay near death. Guilt swept through her.

In a few minutes it was over. Thomas lay still for a moment longer before opening his eyes. He looked at Margaret, and then turned his head away. "You must hate me."

She caressed his cheek. "I can't hate you. You're dear and sweet and precious."

"Do you love me?"

"Please don't ask me that." Disappointment filled his face. She bent down and kissed his forehead. "I have to think. This isn't what I expected to happen today."

"How long do I wait?"

She stood up in silence.

They left the building together and walked north along a path that followed the edge of the bluff. Soon, the beach below vanished and the surf crashed directly into the bluff face.

She held his hands. "I have to go into the village tomorrow, but I'll be here the next day."

"Come away with me. We'll live in a shack and paint all day."

She dropped his hands and turned out to sea. "I can't, Thomas. There are too many people involved."

"I know you're scared of what could happen. I was scared, too, when I brought you that drawing. You could have thrown me out and told me to never come back. But it was worse not to show it to you. I was confused then, but now everything is clear. We're meant to be together. Can't you see that?"

"No, I don't see it. I know you'd like it to be simple but this is very complex. You've only known me for a short while. There are things about me that you can't even guess."

"I know your art, and that is you, the real Margaret. I don't have to

109

know about your past. It doesn't matter."

She looked up to the sky. "Oh, if that were only true. My past follows me everywhere and colors everything I do. I can't run off with you."

"But do you want to?"

The first answer that came to her was *yes*. What she said was, "I don't know."

Without another word, he turned and walked away. Had he guessed that she was lying?

Margaret was quiet that evening at supper. John didn't seem to notice, but Sara asked if she was feeling well. Margaret nodded her head and said that she was just tired.

In the morning Anna drove her and John into Glasen. John seemed oddly chipper as he spoke. "I've set up an interesting interview you might like to attend before tea. One of our fellow countrymen who conducts scientific experiments here. He might warrant a sketch."

Anna drove them to a two-story warehouse that was painted bright red. John knocked. Five minutes passed before a slim, young woman with raven black hair slid open the barn-like door.

John smiled. "Hello. We're the Talbots and we've..."

The woman put her fingers to her lips and whispered. "Shh. You'll disturb his concentration. Follow me. Quietly."

Margaret carried her sketchpad as the woman led them into a cavernous space. The ceiling reached as high as the pitched roof. Windows set high above the floor illuminated a man lying face up on a surgical table. His right hand was on his chest and his left on his brow. He wore a long, white coat over a tweed suit. Bright red hair stuck out in great tufts. Softly, almost imperceptibly, he hummed a tuneless melody.

The woman leaned over to the Talbots and whispered again. "He's trying to solve the problem of news print ink bleed. He's a genius."

The man sat up straight and shouted in a distinctively Midwestern twang. "Of course. Cover each page of the paper in rubber and moisture can't get through. Now, to invent a transparent rubber."

The woman turned to Margaret. "You see? A genius." She walked across the floor. "Dear, we have visitors. The Talbots from New York."

John extended his hand. "Mr. Underwood? I'm John Talbot and this is my wife, Margaret."

Underwood gave a beaming smile as he extended his hand. "Pleased to meet you, Mr. Talbot. Jonah T. Underwood, at your service, sir. The T stands for Tiberius. This is my lovely wife and capable assistant, Morag. So, I understand you write magazine articles of some sort."

"Yes. Have you ever read one of our stories?"

"Don't have time. Always working. Something new to invent every day. Have to keep ahead of that upstart Edison. Inventor indeed. Accountant, huckster, slave keeper. That's what he is. The only thing he ever invented was the repeating telegraph. Everything else was the work of his assistants or was purchased from someone, but do you think they got the credit? No. Even the light bulb that he claims as his masterpiece was invented by someone else—two Canadians from Toronto who sold their patent to Edison for $5,000. He fails to mention that little fact. I had a working electric light a month before anyone else. If I had had a generator here I could have proven it. One of the disadvantages of working in such a remote location."

Margaret tried hard not to laugh as the little, red-headed man waved his arms dramatically in the air. "Then why do you stay here, Mr. Underwood?"

"Ah. You've hit the problem square on the knuckle, as they say. Aside from the fact that I met my beloved here in Glasen and would never think of taking her away from this beauty, I stay for the same reason I came. To invent."

"You couldn't invent where you came from?"

He squinted with one eye as he inspected Margaret. "I like you, Mrs. Talbot. You get right to the heart of the meat. You may find it difficult to believe, considering how well I have blended into the local customs and adopted their mannerisms and speech, but I am not from Glasen."

Margaret felt a giggle coming, but kept it in check. "I would have never guessed."

"I had always wanted to be an inventor, like my father. He invented a machine to make buttons without the need for human intervention, other than to load the machine, run the machine, lubricate the machine, fix it when it broke down which happened several times a day, and unload the completed buttons. Father became a millionaire from the Underwood Button Company. 'Put an Underwood in your underwear.' That was a slogan I made up for him. Tragically, he never had a chance to use it. Fell into one of the machines and was holed to death. Horrible. So I sold the company and followed my idol, Alexander Graham Bell, to Canada. He's a Scot, you know. I'm also a Scot. Well, a fifth at any rate, when you add up both my parents' lineage. All of the great inventors were Scots, unlike Mr. Edison. There's Watt, inventor of the steam engine, and Macintosh, inventor of the rubber raincoat, and..."

Margaret flinched as a deep tone resounded throughout the room. She looked over her shoulder to see Morag standing next to a large gong. Underwood took out his pocket watch. "My word. Is it that time already?" He walked briskly to a ladder that ascended to a platform some thirty feet off the ground. He looked back to the Talbots. "Well, come along. You wanted to see my work, didn't you?" He continued to climb. Margaret looked at John. He shrugged and indicated for her to go first.

On the platform was a wire cage with five seagulls inside. Underwood used a stick to push open a section of the roof. The sun shone brightly through the hole, revealing a blue sky streaked with clouds.

Underwood removed one of the birds and held it in his hand. "Tell me, Mr. Talbot. How much do you know about carrier pigeons?"

"Quite a bit, actually. Margaret and I have used them to send dispatches."

"So you would be able to appreciate the possibilities of a carrier bird that could cross an ocean."

Margaret looked at the gull. "You mean that?"

"Yes, madam. This. An ordinary seagull."

Margaret reached out to touch the closest bird, but drew her hand back quickly when it tried to bite her. "Mr. Underwood. Just how do you propose to train a gull to carry messages to a specific spot?"

Underwood smiled broadly. "By giving the gull the same innate navigational ability of a homing pigeon, that's how. Look at the bottom of the cage. Go on."

Margaret and John looked inside. Long, narrow pieces of metal were laid out in a north, south configuration.

"Magnets," said Underwood. "That's how the homing pigeon can tell where to fly. Its entire body is a compass. By placing these magnets in with the gulls, their bodies will absorb that magnetic ability and they will be able to fly as a pigeon does."

He yelled down to Morag, "Ready with log."

"Log ready."

"Record time."

"8:43 a.m."

"Bird away."

"Bird away."

Underwood released one of the gulls through the hole. It flapped out of the opening and perched on the roof.

Underwood poked at it with a stick. The gull moved aside and settled back down. Underwood shouted down from the platform again, "Make a note. Add two more magnets, and telephone Johnson. No gull today."

"No gull today," came the reply from below.

As they climbed down the ladder, Underwood said, "Science is experimentation. Trial and error. Each failure brings us closer to the truth. We'll get the right number of magnets one day and the world will see global communication. But, let me show you something we're a little closer to. Morag, wheel in the Piceporter."

Morag went into a side room and returned pushing a wheeled table that held two wooden barrels, one large and one small. A three-inch pipe connected them. Three salmon swam around in the larger barrel.

Underwood opened a door to reveal a small steam engine sitting outside. He shoveled some coal into the boiler's firebox, pulled a lever and the flywheel sprang to life. As it did, Margaret noticed that a network of belts and pulleys ran all along the walls.

Underwood attached an idler belt to a pulley on the three-inch pipe.

He raised his voice to be heard over the engine. "This is a fishing village, my friends. The people of Glasen have always made their living from the sea, and always will. There is a great bounty in the ocean, but there is great danger in harvesting it. Each year men go out in their dories, never to return to the arms of their wives and children. It is a fearful toll that the widows of Glasen have been forced to pay year in and year out. That is why I, Jonah T. Underwood, have set all my scientific knowledge and mental capacities to providing that bounty without the price in human lives. Behold. I give you the Piceporter."

Margaret pointed to the table. "Are they going to carry this on their boats?"

Underwood's laugh was nearly lost in the rhythmic pounding of the steam engine. "Oh, no, no, no, Mrs. Talbot. This is only a scale model. The problem, you see, is that men have to go out to sea to bring the fish back here. That's where the danger comes from.

"It would be much better to bring the fish to the men. Imagine, if you would, that the large barrel is the sea and the small one the harbor. Right now, fishermen must row their dories into the big barrel to bring the fish back to the small one. What if the fish could be moved from the big barrel, the sea, to the small barrel, the harbor? The fishermen could just scoop them up with nets and never have to leave dry land.

"That is what the Piceporter does, as represented by this pipe. It sucks the fish right out of the ocean and deposits them in the harbor. Buoys, controlled by cables from shore, would aim it at passing schools. Then, the Piceporter would pull them in and the rest would be net work."

John leaned over to Margaret and whispered, "You know, it might just work." She looked at the strange contraption and raised an eyebrow.

Underwood threw a lever and the belt attached to the Piceporter whirled to life with a whine. Slowly, a swirl of water formed around the lip of the pipe. The swirl became a whirlpool as the fish swam in vain to escape. One was caught in the stream and pulled into the tube. A wrenching grind filled the air and the water in the small barrel turned red as minced chunks of fish spewed into it. Another salmon was sucked up and the sickening rattle again mixed with the banging of the steam engine.

Underwood motioned to Morag who hurried out the door. A moment later the steam engine sputtered to a halt, leaving a ringing in Margaret's ears. She looked into the large barrel where one live salmon swam and then into the smaller one where shredded chunks of fish floated through the water. She felt slightly nauseated, but found it impossible to look away from the macabre sight.

Underwood made some notes. "Of course, there are a few problems to be worked out."

She felt John's arm wrap around hers and heard his voice say, "Thank you, Mr. Underwood. A most interesting demonstration."

She followed his lead out of the building. The inventor shouted after them, "That's U-N-D-E-R-W-O-O-D. Underwood. One fifth Scot, please remember that part. All the great inventors are Scots. Take Alexander Graham Bell, or James Watt. Do call if you have any questions."

As they reached the door she was smiling. Ten steps down the wharf she heard John chuckling. By the time they were twenty paces away they were both laughing uncontrollably. John held her arm tightly and she squeezed his hand.

"Which fifth is the Scot?" she said.

They laughed harder. John shook his head. "I'm not certain, but I think he's sitting on that part right now."

Margaret held her stomach with her free hand. "A few problems?"

John pointed to the roof of the building. "And that stupid bird's still sitting up there." He was laughing so hard she could barely understand him.

It was then that she realized he was touching her. She raised her head and met his eyes. Their laughter slowed, leaving them breathing rapidly as they gazed at one another with wide grins.

John took both of her hands and stared intently into her eyes. He raised one hand to his lips and kissed it gently. She wanted to fling her arms around him, tell him how much she still loved him, still wanted him, but she was afraid to act, lest she break the magic of the instant.

He said, "May I walk you to Mrs. Gunn's house?"

Margaret nodded her head. John took her arm in his once more and they set off at a leisurely pace.

CHAPTER EIGHT

Mrs. Gunn met them at the door. John paid his respects and then excused himself. Margaret wished she could run after him to hold him close and bury her head in his chest. She told herself that there would be plenty of time for that tonight and every night.

Margaret was ushered into the parlor where six other women waited. Mrs. Gunn made the introductions. "You know Mrs. Lamont, of course, and I'm sure you remember Mrs. Patterson."

"I certainly do."

"And this is Mrs. McRae, Mrs. Ross, Mrs. Douglas, and her daughter, Catherine. Ladies, I am so pleased to present Mrs. Margaret Talbot."

Tea and cake were served. Margaret complimented Mrs. Gunn on her dress and Catherine on the cake that she had baked. The ten-year-old girl grinned as she blushed. All the while, Margaret kept picturing the smile on John's face.

She told of her journeys around the world as her audience sat with wide eyes. They followed every word about the African savannah and the steppes of Asia, the beauty of Paris and the wonder of Venice. All the while, John was in each tale.

Mrs. Gunn brought out the copy of *The Wide World Magazine* that she had bought at the Lamont Brothers' store and Margaret went over each illustration from China and explained how she had come to draw them.

Margaret brought out some sketches. Everyone was delighted with her drawings of Fr. Williams, the store, the wharf, and the *Scarlet Lion*.

Mrs. Gunn fanned herself. "What an amazing life you have led to see all that. I hope my Andy can see as many places. He's working at the new steel plant in Sydney and is saving his money to travel the world."

"That sounds very exciting."

Mrs. Gunn hesitated for an instant before saying, "Yes. It is."

"How long has he been gone?"

"Three years, now. He writes regularly and sends a little money home from his pay. He's a good boy. In his last letter he said he wanted to come home for Christmas."

Margaret smiled. "That will be nice."

Mrs. Gunn formed a smile, but the edges of her lips turned down. She took out a handkerchief to blot her eyes. "*Tha mi amaid.*"

Anna said, "You are not a fool, Elly."

Mrs. Gunn smiled at Anna. "Thank you." She looked back to Margaret. "Please forgive me. You see, Andy's written home every year since left with a promise to come home for Christmas. He never has. He never will. Once they leave Glasen, they don't come back."

Anna said, "There's nothing left to hold them here. The timber fetches a meager price and the fish less. The last time I saw my youngest daughter was nearly a decade ago when Alistair and I traveled to Boston to visit with her and her husband. I haven't seen my oldest girl in twenty years."

Margaret felt a sudden pain in her belly at the memory of losing her own child. "I'm so sorry. I had no idea."

Mrs. Gunn said, "There's no need for sorrow. They've gone on to something better. That's what we really want for them, after all."

Goodbyes were exchanged. Anna fetched the surrey. Margaret

held Mrs. Gunn's hand. "Thank you so much for inviting me. I had a wonderful time. I hope your son does come back for Christmas."

Mrs. Gunn squeezed Margaret's hand. "Thank you."

On the ride back, Margaret recalled the stories she had told at tea and remembered John in each adventure.

Anna said, "Alistair and I were wondering if the two of you would like to come over to supper on Thursday?"

"That would be wonderful, Anna." She sat back against the seat and smiled. Large, fluffy clouds floated overhead in a sunny sky.

Anna looked over to her. "You're quite cheerful."

Margaret drew a deep, clear breath of air. "I was just thinking about how marvelous life is."

The next day dawned bright. Margaret spread her sketches across the dining room table in the Grants' house, but was unable to concentrate on any of them. Her mouth turned up into a grin. It was ridiculous, she told herself. John had merely taken her arm as they walked to Mrs. Gunn's. When he left this morning, he had smiled at her in a way he hadn't for years.

Sara came in from the kitchen with a basket of herbs. She twirled three times, set the basket on the table, and clapped her hands together. "Oh, you're happy today. You should smile all the time."

Margaret covered her mouth with her fingers and tried not to giggle. "What have you been gathering?"

Sara picked up the basket and walked into the kitchen. "I don't know their names. They're just things that make the food taste good."

At first, Margaret worried that Sara might have inadvertently gathered something poisonous. She reminded herself that Ian had been eating Sara's cooking since she had arrived and showed no harm from it.

Margaret placed the drawings into a portfolio. "I'm going out for a walk, Sara. I just can't concentrate on this anymore."

"More Muse?"

Margaret smiled and said, "Yes," feeling that at least this time she wasn't lying.

———

She walked into the deep woods next to the Grants' house, her thoughts focused on John as a giddy excitement ran through her. Her mind turned to the portrait of Blossom. Would John's change extend to her painting?

A sudden desire to see the portrait consumed her. Carefully, she walked to the carriage house and climbed the steps to the loft. As she did, she thought of Thomas. She had not spoken to him since John's change of attitude. So much had happened and she could not imagine what she was going to say to him.

She climbed the stairs and saw Thomas's portrait of her standing on an easel. The eyes caught her at once. No longer sketches, they were full and complete. She could see they had been reworked many times. It was like staring into a mirror that reflected what she tried to hide. Here was the strength she had wanted to give Blossom. Yet there was more. Pain, exhaustion, longing, and something that left her stomach cold. Desperation. His technique was subtle. The eyes slightly downcast, the lids barely closed, the gaze steady but unfocused. A work masterful in its simplicity.

A flash of movement caught her eye and she turned to see Thomas standing off to one side of the loft.

He said, "They're your eyes, Margaret. The eyes I can't get out of my mind." He stepped forward and took her hand. "I had to finish them before they drove me mad."

"Thomas. You shouldn't have come up here."

"Sara didn't see me." He put his arms around her. She stepped back and saw confusion on his face.

He shook his head. "What's wrong?"

She wanted to run down the stairs and into the woods, and keep on running until she dropped. "Thomas, I like you very much. I don't want anything to happen to you."

"I like *you*. I love you."

She blinked back tears. "Thomas, this can't go on."

"What do you mean?"

119

"It's not right. It's not ethical. I need to be just your teacher again."

"I know what you need. You need to be loved. You want to be loved, and your husband will never give you that. I will."

She sat on a crate. "No, Thomas. John took my hand yesterday. He walked with me and he... He's my husband, Thomas. Can't you see?"

His face hardened. "I see, all right. The big city woman wanted to have a little fun with the local cripple."

"No, Thomas. You know that's not true."

"Well, did you have a good time? Did you have your thrill or is everything just a bore to you?"

Margaret reached out to touch him, but he sprang away from her. "You're nothing but a bitter old woman who has to use people to feel alive. Well, go to hell. I don't need you. I don't need anyone." He dashed down the stairs.

Margaret sat on the crate. "Oh God, what have I done?" She had to talk to someone. She thought at first of Anna, then Fr. Williams, but felt she could say nothing to either. A large cloud passed overhead, cutting off the sun. The portrait of her was thrown into shadow, but the eyes remained bright.

She stood motionless until a rasping sound filtered into the building. Margaret went to the round window on the gable end and looked outside. At the edge of the bluff, Sara stood next to a seal. When it barked she laughed and nodded her head as if in conversation.

The seal stopped and looked out to sea. It made a shrill sound and turned back to Sara. Her smile fell into a somber expression. She looked to the seal, then out to the sea, and then, with a long turn, back to the house she shared with Ian. For several minutes she stared at the little salt-box before turning back to the seal and shaking her head slowly.

The seal raised its head and gave one bark before scooting away across the bluff and down the stairs to the dock. Sara watched in silence.

As the seal swam out into the water and dove beneath the waves, Margaret experienced an inexplicable desire to accompany it into the ocean. The feeling lasted for only an instant. She left the loft and walked into the woods.

She returned to the house an hour later. It was alive with the warm, comforting smell of bread baking. Sara came skipping out of the kitchen. "Oh, you're back. Now we can bake together. I love baking and feeling the dough between my fingers." She took Margaret by the hands and danced in a circle. Margaret found herself laughing. It just seemed impossible to do otherwise.

She released Sara's hands. "What are you baking?"

Sara pursed one side of her mouth. "Let's see. I took out three loaves of bread. That should be enough for tonight. I just put the scones in, but we still have to make the pies."

Margaret wrung her hands together. "Sara, I need to talk to somebody about something."

"All right."

"It's rather hard to talk about."

"Do you have trouble pronouncing words, too?"

"No. It's very complicated."

"Is it about wagons? I find them very complicated. I still don't understand how the wheels go around."

It seemed more productive to talk to a tree and Margaret was about to give up when a look of recognition crossed Sara's face. "Oh," the young woman said. "An inside hard thing."

Margaret nodded her head.

Sara led Margaret into the parlor and guided her to the sofa. Margaret twisted her hands. "Sara, I've done a terrible thing." Stopping occasionally to gather her resolve, Margaret told Sara about the growing rift between her and John, the friendship with Thomas that had gone further than she had intended, John's sudden kindness, and Thomas's outburst. She carefully kept her use of the carriage house a secret.

Sara sat silently, her eyes fixed on Margaret.

At the end of the tale Sara said, "I understand sadness, but I still do not understand hurt. You are all nice people. I don't know why everyone can't be happy."

"It's not that easy. Everyone wants something different."

Sara stared at her, and then laughed. "I understand now. You really think that's true." She stopped laughing. "Oh, but that's sad. You don't know what you want."

Margaret felt anger rising in her. "Of course I know what I want. I want to paint. I want John to love me again. I want Thomas to..." Images and desires flooded her mind; the freedom to paint, her baby alive, critical acclaim, Robert Henri's approval, John's approval. She asked herself what any of that meant and what it would actually feel like. With a start, she realized that she didn't know. She couldn't even say for certain how she would know if someone loved her.

Even though they were indoors, she smelled salt spray. She found herself sitting on the sofa with Sara's arms cradling her. The confusion subsided as Margaret went limp. She snuggled into Sara's embrace and listened to her hum another tune that was so familiar, yet completely new. Margaret let herself be rocked. She had no idea what time it was or when Ian and John would be back. She didn't care. She just rocked and listened to the music of the sea.

Like a mist dispersing, the grief and fear dissolved, though a sense of something unfinished remained. She sat up. Sara stared at her intently. This young woman did not seem so young anymore.

Sara said, "You carry too much yesterday inside you. That is how Ian was when I first came. He had to let it out for me to stay. It was hard for him because he keeps his pain to himself. He said things in anger that were echoes from the past, but they had to be given voice before he could let them go. Some still remain locked in the carriage house. One day, they too will go."

Mention of the carriage house made Margaret wince. "I didn't mean to hurt Thomas. I don't want to hurt anyone."

"I know, Margaret. You're a good person. You're just confused. So is John and so is Thomas. All of you hold tightly to your yesterdays. You've all forgotten what's really important."

CHAPTER NINE

When John returned from the village, he again took Margaret's hands in his. A sense of euphoria rose in her. Then she remembered Sara's words from earlier in the afternoon about Ian having to let his anger have voice before he could release it. A cold shiver ran down her back. It lasted only a moment, but it colored the rest of the evening.

In the middle of the night, sour bile tore her from sleep. She tried to relax, but her mind swirled with questions for which no answers came; why had John refused to touch her for so long? What happened to the baby? Had there been a proper burial? Would she be allowed to paint openly? Was she even able to call herself an artist with the failure of Blossom's portrait? What did she truly want? No answers came to her.

She squirmed as she tried to find a comfortable position. Each hour dragged into the next and still the questions bombarded her. She finally fell asleep just before dawn.

She dreamed she was in the hospital. Her arms and legs were tied to the bed with ropes. Two doctors stood next to her, their faces concealed by masks. A nurse came into the room with a baby in her arms. Margaret knew it was hers. The nurse grasped the newborn by one leg and dangled the child over the bed. The baby cried and Margaret fought to break free of the ropes. She screamed for the nurse to leave the baby alone. One of the doctors removed his mask to reveal John's face. She pleaded for him to save their child but he looked away as if he hadn't heard.

She woke and sat upright. Her hands shook as she looked over at John, who still lay asleep next to her. She fought an urge to wake him and demand answers to the questions that had kept her awake. She told herself that it was another time. It was over and best forgotten. He loved her again. Pressing on him now could destroy everything. She fell back asleep with no further nightmares.

At dawn, John got dressed and walked downstairs. Margaret closed her eyes. When she opened them again, it was half-past ten.

She felt groggy all morning. As she worked, the questions from the night before distracted her. She forced herself to concentrate on the sketches. By mid-afternoon she fought to keep her eyes open. The exhaustion won and she fell asleep at the table.

The next night brought another dream. In it, John pulled the baby from her arms and handed the infant to a doctor. She woke to cold sweats. It was before dawn. Quietly, she got dressed and went downstairs to the parlor to sit on the sofa.

She stared silently off into the darkness. The room was still filled with shadows when she heard Sara come downstairs to begin breakfast. Ian descended a few minutes later. Neither of them noticed her.

Sara's voice floated in from the dining room. "The south bank is barren today. The fish think they are clever. They will all go to that shoal to the east."

Ian gave a deep, "Hmm." When Margaret heard the scrape of his chair being pushed back from the table, she got up and peeked around the corner. Ian stood in the kitchen, illuminated by lamp light. He wore his rain slicker and sou'wester. Sara kissed him gently on the lips. He took her hand in his and kissed her fingers. A moment later, he was out the door.

Margaret scurried back to the parlor and sat down again. First light arrived. The features of the room grew slowly out of diffused shapes as the chairs, the tables, and the fireplace changed from gray to muted colors.

Things had all seemed so clear at Mrs. Gunn's tea party. Now, nothing made sense. It was as if a wall inside her held something back. She could feel the pressure of it, and even though she didn't know what it was, she was certain she didn't like it.

The words of John's poem moved through her mind. She had to be the one he was protecting, but she could not imagine what she was being protected from, or what duty he felt.

The memory of the dreams and the poem refused to go away. She rubbed her forehead with her fingers as a headache grew. *I have no time for this.* There were sketches to finish and Blossom's portrait needed work. This caused her to think of Thomas, and the bile in her stomach rose again.

The thump of John's footsteps came down the stairs and echoed into the dining room. He said, "Good morning Sara. Have you seen Margaret?"

Sara's musical voice greeted him. "She hasn't come in for breakfast yet. Would you like some? There's porridge and I can make pancakes, or anything else you want."

"Porridge will be fine, thank you."

Margaret got up and ambled into the dining room. John looked up with a smile. "Good morning. Have you been up long?"

She sat down across from him without replying.

John said, "I'll be speaking with Phillip Lamont. Do you want anything sent over?"

"Such as?"

"I don't know. Paper. Toiletries."

She kept her gaze on the table. "No."

"If you change your mind, let me know." He reached over and placed his hand over hers and looked out the window. "What a beautiful day. I could come back early and we could have a picnic, just the two of us."

Sara emerged like a fury with porridge and muffins, pancakes, honey, and smoked salmon. John ate heartily as Sara looked on, asking if everything was all right and if he liked it. "Not everyone cares for salmon. If you don't like it I've got fish cakes."

John swallowed. "Sara, this is wonderful. I couldn't think of anything else I would want to eat right now."

She smiled and went back into the kitchen. Margaret stared at the table.

John said, "Are you feeling all right?"

She pushed her chair back and shot to her feet. "You bastard. My baby is dead, your baby, and you left me to die in that hospital bed without even holding my hand."

John nearly fell out of his chair.

Margaret clenched her fists and struggled to speak. "I was so scared and you left me to die. You bastard. And then, you put me through hell for the last two years. Why? Do you despise me? Have you grown tired of me?"

A knock came at the door. Sara appeared from the kitchen, giving no indication she had heard anything, and welcomed Anna Lamont inside.

"Hello Sara, Mr. Talbot, Margaret."

John stood up, his face blanched. "Good morning, Anna."

Sara shifted her weight from side to side, a smile on her face. "Are you staying for some pancakes? I've just made a new batch."

"No, dear, I've already eaten."

Margaret wanted to be far away where she could scream for hours when Anna said, "Are you ready, Margaret?"

Margaret fought to keep her voice calm. "Ah..."

"I hope that you are still coming to supper tonight."

Margaret had completely forgotten about the invitation. She could not imagine herself visiting anyone right then, yet, she found herself mechanically saying, "Of course. I've been looking forward to it."

Anna smiled. "Wonderful. I'll be back around five."

John placed the box that held his pens and ink into a satchel along with some paper and walked toward the front door. He looked back at Margaret. A part of her felt relieved by the outburst, as if an old cramp had relaxed in her gut. At the same time, she had no idea why she had lashed out when things were going so well. Before she could think of something to say, John turned and left.

Sara returned from the kitchen. Margaret's stomach churned and she pushed the food away.

After Sara cleared the table, Margaret absently cleaned up some sketches of the village and tried not to think of Thomas or John. The more she worked, the worse the drawings became until she finally gave up.

Sara came into the dining room with a wide-brimmed hat in her hands. "I promised to walk down the road to visit Mrs. Oman. Would you like to come? She makes the most wonderful cakes."

"Thank you, but I think I'll just stay here."

Margaret waited fifteen minutes before going outside to the carriage house. She carefully pulled the rear door open and climbed the steps to the loft.

She set out tubes of paint and brushes. Thomas's painting stood to the side. Margaret studied it and considered what she would say to him before realizing she would never have that chance.

For all the conflict and confusion pulling at her, a deep sense of professional duty forced her to look at his work clearly. For all his gift of drawing, he had a great deal of work to do. More, he needed patience to master a craft which, unlike drawing, did not come naturally to him. Still, there was something in the eyes of the painting, a sense of sadness, that she had tried so hard to keep secret.

Blossom's portrait was in another corner. Margaret positioned it in the center of the loft where the light from the half oval window shone brightly on it. She refused to believe it was a self-portrait. Blossom was her guide. Blossom had endured. Margaret would endure.

She found the sketches that she had made in the sharecropper's shack and traced a finger over the page. "How did you do it? How did you bury your babies without burying yourself?" The more Margaret searched, the further she seemed to be from any answers. Even in the sketches, the arms had lost all strength. They were simply exhausted.

"Damn." Margaret scattered the drawings across the floor. "You're going to be strong, Blossom, whether you like it or not." With a trowel knife she forcefully scraped the painted arms off of the canvas and began again. She mixed paint on the pallet and took a narrow, flat brush in hand. Holding it at arm's length, she transcended the outburst with John, the affections of Thomas, the antics of Sara, and methodically applied paint, stepped back to inspect her work, and moved forward again to apply more paint.

Over and over the dance went. A rhythm formed as Margaret gave into a near trance. Lighter brown gave a shimmer to one vein on of arm. A tingle ran up Margaret's back. The top of the arm rose light and airy as it reached up. This was it. She could sense that special something that had eluded her. It was almost there. Blossom, strong, commanding, unbeaten. One more highlight.

She ran a line across the bottom of the same arm to create contrast. It seemed to burn with dark fire and gave the impression that the arm sagged. She scraped off the paint and applied it fresh. The arm seemed to fall lower and Blossom's expression took on a sense of desperation.

Margaret threw the brush to the ground. She looked to the eyes in Thomas's painting of her and back to Blossom's. They held the same expression. "Damn."

After cleaning up, Margaret eased her way down from the loft and out of the carriage house. The strong odor of cooking fat permeated the air. She came around the corner to see Sara standing between the house and the well. Three large iron kettles stood next to her. Fires burned beneath two of them. A wooden table held some bags and knives. Sara stirred the kettle closest to the well with a large wooden paddle. Margaret couldn't imagine how the lithe woman had wrestled them into place.

Sara waved. "I'm making soap."

Margaret put a handkerchief to her nose. "I didn't think anyone still made their own soap."

"Oh, we can buy it, of course, but Ian prefers the homemade kind."

"I guess he grew up with it."

Sara shook her head with a chuckle. "Ian had the finest soaps in his yesterday time."

The ornate carriage and the box of photographs came to Margaret's mind. "Where did Ian grow up?"

"That was before I knew him. Don't be put off by the smell. This is the worst part, cooking the fat down. At least it's from sheep. Beef tallow is unbearable. I'll add some flowers to make it sweet and fresh."

Margaret decided not to pursue the subject of Ian's past for the moment. "How long does this take?"

"The cooking part takes an hour or so. Then, things have to cool for an hour. That's enough time to have lunch. The final steps take another hour."

Margaret found herself curious as to how soap was made. Her mother had always traded eggs for soap. Besides, she told herself, it would take her mind off of things she would rather not think about. "Can I help?"

"Yes. If you take over stirring I can prepare the next step."

"All right, but wait just a moment."

Margaret ran inside the house and grabbed a sketchbook and a pencil. Once back outside, she made a quick drawing of Sara at the pot. It was thrilling to feel control over a medium again. When she finished three sketches she tossed the book on the ground and clasped the handle of the paddle.

Sara's demeanor took on a serious air. She measured out ingredients with the precision of a chemist, all the while with a look of grave concentration.

Sara laid out a handkerchief on the table and opened a glass jar. With a spoon, she ladled out a pile of crystals. She tied the ends of the handkerchief together. "I buy the lye mail order from the Eaton's catalogue. Most people use sodium hydroxide, but I prefer potassium hydroxide because it keeps the soap soft longer, even though it has a more violent reaction when added to water, so be careful."

Margaret was taken aback by Sara's use of such precise scientific terms, something that was completely unlike her. It was another puzzle that Margaret could not answer.

When the fat had melted, they strained it through cheesecloth, washed it in cold water and added a small handful of salt.

Margaret sat the empty bucket down. "What now?"

"We wait for it to cool. That will take about an hour. Meanwhile, we can have a nice lunch."

The young woman prepared a basket of food and took it, along with a table cloth and a pitcher of cool water, out onto the moss-covered mound halfway to the road. They sat down and had a fine meal of cheese, cold mutton, and fresh blueberries.

A shape moved in the forest across the road. "Sara, I think Beth Ramsey is over there in the woods on the hill across the road."

Sara looked across the road. "Beth Ramsay, is that you? Won't you come and join our picnic?"

Beth Ramsey's voice came faint across the distance. "I'll nay come under the power o' you witches."

Sara turned to Margaret. "We'll just have to let her stay. She can be up there all day."

Margaret said, "Doesn't she ever get tired of this?"

"When I first came to Glasen she was up there most every day, and some nights. Ian put a stop to it. She fears him more than goblins."

"You canna make me come down. I know what you're up to."

Margaret cupped her hands and shouted up the hill. "You had best be gone, Beth Ramsey. It's my birthday, and Ian's coming home for lunch to celebrate. We're just waiting for him. Do you want him to find you here?"

With a rustling of leaves, Beth Ramsey rolled out of the woods and onto the road some fifty feet away. She got up and shook her fist. "You'll regret this. I'll... I'll..." Seeming to lack a sufficient reply, she waddled off toward Glasen.

Sara looked to Margaret with a quizzical look. "You never said it was your birthday."

Margaret laughed. "It isn't, and Ian isn't coming to lunch."

"You lied?"

"It got rid of her, didn't it?"

"She likes the game. You didn't have to lie."

There was painful look in Sara's eyes and Margaret felt a sense of guilt. She wanted to explain that the lie hadn't meant anything and that the end result justified it. All the lies she had told since arriving in Glasen tumbled together and the weight of them left a lump in her throat.

"I'm sorry Sara. Sometimes people where I come from tell small lies to get someone to do something or to try to not hurt their feelings."

"You mean like telling Anna you had looked forward to supper all week when you had actually forgotten about it?"

Margaret froze. "How did you know I had forgotten?"

"It was on your face."

Margaret worried about what else Sara could see on her face. "I'm sorry about that, too."

Sara thought for a moment. "You come from a very strange place if people have to lie to each other to not hurt someone's feelings. It's very sad, and I think I understand better the sadness you and John feel. It's always on your faces." Then she jumped up and danced in a little circle. "Well, the tallow has had time to cool. Let's make soap."

Sara used a knife to scrape the fat from on top of the water and placed it into one of the pots. "It's good and clean." When she was done, she put the cast-iron pot over the flames. Margaret again marveled at how easily Sara maneuvered it.

Sara said, "Now, put in about a quarter of the lye."

Margaret picked up the handkerchief. As she added the crystals of lye, she held it at arm's length as she remembered Sara's warning about burning. Indeed, the lye popped and spit as it was dumped into the water. She got her hand too close and gave a yelp when some of the lye water splashed on her fingers. It left no mark but it stung for several minutes.

Sara finished the next steps. Finally the soap was left to cool overnight. Sara picked up a basket. "I have to gather the flowers for tomorrow. Would you like to come?"

Margaret was tempted, but had a sudden urge to work on Blossom's portrait again. She began to form an elaborate excuse in her head about having to complete some sketches before John got back, but could not bring herself to lie to Sara again. She simply said, "No. I'll just stay here."

"All right. I may not see you before you leave for supper. Have a good time."

"Thank you."

Sara walked south, down the road, basket in hand, and Margaret heard her sing one of her nonsense tunes. The melody was uplifting and drove the guilt from Margaret's mind. As Sara rounded the corner, the tune faded away.

Margaret noticed there was still some lye crystals left in the handkerchief. She wasn't sure it was safe to just leave them on the table, so she folded them up in the handkerchief and placed it in the pocket of her skirt before heading for the loft.

She opened the door and climbed the stairs. Standing in the middle of the loft was Thomas Brown. Neither of them spoke for several minutes. Why he had come back? If he intended to hurt her, she could do little to fight against his strength. With no one around for miles she could not even call for help. She kept her gaze on Thomas and wondered where the pallet knife was.

Thomas hung his head. "You must hate me."

A cold ache filled her chest. "Oh Thomas, I don't hate you."

He cried openly, his voice a whisper between sobs. "I'm so ashamed. I had no right to say those things."

She started to go to him, but forced herself to remain in place. "I'm the one who should be ashamed. I could see what was happening, and I should have stopped it. I should have been stronger. It is I who betrayed you."

He pulled at his hair with both hands. "I should never have said anything to you. I wish I had never felt any of this."

She went to him now, taking his hands and holding them tightly. "Never say that, Thomas. Never apologize for what you feel. Even in pain, relish the passion of who you are. We are different than other people, you and I. We are artists. We feel things other people never will, with intensity others will never experience. We can't shut those feelings off. They are what we draw; our art from. We have to use them. Do you understand?"

His face was contorted as he cried. "I just want to learn to paint. Please. Take me back as your student. I've seen what I can be and I can't return to what I was."

She put her arms around him and they both cried. Wiping her eyes, she stepped back and took a deep breath. "Painting is more than colors and brushes. Those things are just mechanics. Art is what you do with them to express your soul. You have to look into yourself to discover what you will express. There can be no compromise in this. You have just seen how hard it can be. Do you want to go on?"

He stared out the oval window. "How do I keep from feeling how I feel abou' you?"

"You can't."

He turned to her. "Then I should leave."

"Is that what you want?"

"No."

"No because of how you feel about me, or no because you want to be an artist?"

"I want to be an artist, and I want to be near you because of how I feel. I don't see how I can have both."

As he spoke, she could clearly see the bright, artistic spark inside him. He could be taught, molded. He deserved it. She owed it to him.

"I'm going to teach you to paint, Thomas. I'm going to teach you technique and I'm going to teach you to direct your feelings. You are going to learn discipline. It is what you want and what you are destined to have."

She knew she could direct him and not hurt him again. There were enough sketches for two articles. All of her time could be directed to Thomas and Blossom.

A thought floated through the back of her mind. *The boy still loves me. I've broken with John. What will I do when Thomas touches me again?* She had no answer.

Thomas studied his portrait of Margaret as she set out paint and brushes. She came over and stood behind him. "You have the eyes. They're the focus. Everything is drawn to them. But they're not finished. They're my eyes, Thomas. Frighteningly so. What's missing are yours. Your view of me. I am merely a model here. As the artist, you must express your interpretation of me. Otherwise it is merely an exercise in mechanics. Ultimately, all art is self-portrait."

Thomas turned. "Pose nude for me."

Margaret's tried to ignore his request. "You need to concentrate on the eyes first."

"Please. It's how I see you, Free of clothes and all they mean. Free."

"Thomas, I don't…"

"It's my view of you. My interpretation."

There was nothing puritanical or shocking to Margaret about the naked form. She had taken life classes when she studied under Robert Henri at the School of Design for Women in Philadelphia. Some of the students, including herself, had taken turns modeling nude for each other. Still, she told herself it was too dangerous to tempt Thomas and herself. She tried to form the word *no*, but she found herself mute.

Thomas said, "Please, Margaret. I'll paint you that way if you pose or not. Didn't you tell me Robert Henri once said, 'Don't only paint a shell of a thing?' Would you have me create truth or lies?"

The word lie cut into her. She asked herself if she could lie again. Still, what would happen if John found out? They had made a commitment to their editor to stay through the first change of the autumn colors. That was weeks away. The loft was a safe place. But if John learned of Thomas' portrait of her, she would lose her only place to paint.

"All right, Thomas. I'll pose for you. But I am still your instructor. You will listen to every critique I give you and perform every exercise. At the same time, I will be your model, and nothing more. You are not to construe anything else between us. Is that understood?"

"Yes."

She wished there was a screen to disrobe behind, but there was nothing. Slowly, she undressed, purposefully averting her eyes from Thomas.

It was only when she was utterly naked that she looked to Thomas with a sense of disappointment as she found him studying the canvas and not looking at her at all. She picked up the clothes and placed them carefully across a wooden crate.

Thomas looked up. "Please remove your hair pin." He went back to mixing paint.

Slowly, she reached up and drew out the pin. Her blond hair fell in fine strands across her shoulders and down her back. "How would you like me to pose?"

Thomas sat the pallet down and looked around the loft as he ran his right hand over his chin. He paused and smiled before dragging an empty trunk into the center of the loft. "Please. Sit here."

He looked around and settled his gaze on her skirt. "This will do." He draped it half over her. "We'll pretend it's a robe." He arranged the garment, leaving one breast and a thigh exposed.

He stepped back. "Yes. You're an artist's model. It's just before class and you're waiting, as you have many times, to sit unemotionally before strangers. You hardly see them anymore, just vague shapes at the edge of vision.

"Once, it excited you to sit on that stool, the center of everyone's attention. Now, it's become mechanical—a way to buy food. But today, as you wait, you stare past everyone and everything and think abou' the life you really want and what it is that truly matters to you. Yes. That's it. Hold that pose."

Margaret could only catch a glimpse of him in her peripheral vision. It grew hot in the loft. A sheen of sweat formed on her skin. Thomas paused to remove his shirt.

As he worked, her mind wandered. She thought about her own painting, about making soap with Sara and about the sketches she last worked on. All the while, she stared ahead at the oval window and lost track of time.

As Thomas worked, she began to think about what he had said. She could imagine just such a young woman, doing what she had to in the hope of achieving what she wanted. She knew some people who would call it a betrayal of principles, prostitution without sex. Was she so different? For years, she had produced the magazine drawings and painted when she could, all with the highest hopes. Years of compromise with no results to show.

What do I want now? she asked herself. *To paint* came the answer without hesitation. It was not the money, which rarely came to artists, nor was it truly fame, though recognition and respect were bound in the dream. She had wanted this as a student of Robert Henri and she still wanted it. But as she stared out the window, she realized that, both then and now, she also wanted to be loved and be in love.

She asked herself if she really did want love after what she had said to John. Was John the only one who could love her? The more the ideas rolled about in her head, the less likely it seemed that she would be able to paint and find love. There would always be a compromise and she hated the thought of it.

At that moment she heard John's voice calling from outside. "Margaret? Where are you?"

She pulled the skirt close to her naked body. Thomas stood silently, looking toward her. She walked quietly to him and whispered in his ear. "I'll dress and go downstairs. Clean up quietly. Wait half an hour before leaving. Can you do that?"

He nodded his head. She wasn't certain why, but she kissed him on the cheek. As she did, one of her naked breasts brushed against his bare chest. He reached out and held her by the waist. Neither moved until Thomas took her hand and gently kissed it.

Margaret quickly dressed and checked to make certain John was not in sight as she exited the carriage house. She adjusted her clothing before walking around the corner.

John came up from the stairs that lead down to the ocean. "Where have you been?"

"I was walking in the woods to the north, along the bluffs. I just couldn't work anymore and had to clear my head."

He eyed her for a moment and Margaret was certain he was

trying to gauge her mood. "Alistair is waiting in the parlor to take us to dinner. Are you ready?"

Margaret had intended to change for dinner after having made soap with Sara earlier. Now, she was afraid that asking for time to do so would only lead to suspicions. "I'm quite ready. Let's go."

CHAPTER TEN

Anna waved as Alistair drove the surrey up to the Lamont's house. "I'm so glad to see you."

When they were all inside, Anna made straight for the kitchen.

Margaret called after her, "Can I help?"

Anna waved one hand over her head and continued moving. "No, no. I won't be a minute."

Alistair led them into the parlor and eased his rotund frame into a chair with a well-settled cushion. "I hear you've had a word or two with young Thomas Brown, Mrs. Talbot."

Margaret was certain both men could see her blushing. "I've looked at a few more of his drawings and made some suggestions."

John said, "You never mentioned seeing him."

"He stopped by the Grants' house. I didn't think you would be interested." Her words sounded forced to her ears. She turned casually to Alistair. "He's very talented. I hope he finds his way to an art school someday."

Alistair lit a cigar. "I'm afraid that will never happen, and all the pity for it. As you say, he has a rare talent. I'd like to see him go to school. I'd be willing to pay for his room and board. Many in Glasen would happily do the same."

John said, "What keeps him from going?"

"It's his fits. He could never have anyone outside the village see them. At least he's known here. Out there, he's afraid he'd be nothing but a freak."

Anna entered the parlor regally. "Dinner is served."

Dinner consisted of a roast, potatoes, carrots and bread. As with the lamb at Phillip's house, everything was wonderful. Margaret found herself thrilled at the change from seafood. When they were through she said, "Anna, you must have spent all day cooking."

"Oh, the roast mostly cooks itself and the other things don't take much fussing."

Alistair wiped his mouth with his napkin. "Just from eight this morning until you arrived."

Anna dabbed her mouth. "Pshaw."

They all laughed. John pushed himself back from the table. "Well, I for one am filled to the point of contentment."

Alistair likewise pressed his abundant girth away from the table and stood. "My good wife. That was an outstanding meal, and it fares all the better for the company. John, would you care to join me in the parlor for some brandy and cigars?"

"I would be delighted."

Margaret felt indignation rise at John's acceptance of an invitation that clearly excluded her and Anna, along with the men's unspoken expectation that the two women would clean up.

She considered making a scene and embarrassing both of them, but realized it would also embarrass Anna. Fighting to hold her anger in, she helped remove the dirty dishes and serving plates to the kitchen where Anna was pumping water into a sink. "Thank you so much for helping, Margaret. I really do appreciate it."

"Of course. I'm only too happy to help, and very glad you invited us."

"Well, you and your husband are a real treat for us. You bring tales from places Alistair and I will never see. Our youngest daughter married a man who captains a steam ship. His home port is Boston, but he's been all over the world. We have post cards from everywhere. He's gone from home for months at a time. My daughter's still waiting to learn if he'll be back for Christmas."

The clock struck eight. Anna looked out a window to a growing twilight. "It's getting dark sooner." She lit an oil lamp and returned to the dishes.

Margaret finished drying a plate. "Anna, have you ever noticed how much time we spend waiting for men?"

"What do you mean, dear?"

"Your daughter's waiting to learn if her husband will come home for Christmas. We're waiting for John and Alistair to finish their odious cigars and drink their brandy." She recalled an assignment from before the stillbirth. "Do you like brandy?"

"Oh, heavens, I've never even tasted it."

"I have. There was a night on the Russian steppes. John was already asleep. I sat in a tent with Cossacks swapping lies and drinking; brandy, whisky, cognac, strong coffee. They told me I was tough and had accepted me into their fraternity. One of the men finished a story about galloping across the steppes while carrying a defeated enemy's head and howling at the moon."

She laughed in remembrance. "I told him I would like to see that, as if I were calling his bluff. He smiled broadly through teeth stained by tobacco and asked whose head I'd like him to carry. They all laughed. I had said he could carry his own, which brought even more laughter, but that I'd only wanted to see him galloping at night and howling at the moon.

"So, they found a pair of pantaloons for me, saying I'd have to ride with them, and they put me on the back of a horse. We took off with our heads full of hot liquor, the wild wind in our faces, and galloped in the dark. Then, full and bright, the moon rose over the horizon. We all howled like mad and dangerous fiends."

Margaret paused and looked out the window. "It was the most foolhardy thing I've ever done. If my horse had stepped in a hole out there in the dark, I'd have probably broken my neck." She turned back to Anna. "But for that instant, I was never more alive."

"Oh my gosh. What did John say?"

Margaret laughed. "I've never told him. The next morning my head pounded so fiercely I was inclined to think the whole thing was a bad dream. But I really knew better." She grabbed Anna by the hand. "It's a full moon tonight. Let's go howl at it."

Anna tried to extricate herself. "I don't know."

"Come on. We'll ride out into the forest and howl. It's great. You'll see."

"Well..."

"It'll pay those two men back for excluding us from their stinky cigars and dull talk."

As independent as Anna had described herself in her youth, she hesitated a long time. Then, she let the plate she was washing slip back into the sink and dried her hands. "All right. Let's go howl."

There was a bottle of sherry on the dining room sideboard. Margaret picked it up along with two glasses. She and Anna walked past the parlor where the men talked and sipped brandy between long draws on cigars.

Alistair looked up. "Where are you two off to?"

Anna started to mutter a reply when Margaret took her arm and hurried them both along. "Out." She caught the two men lowering their heads conspiratorially.

The leaves had begun their transformation from multi-hues of greens to a patchwork of yellows, oranges, and reds as the evenings had turned progressively cooler. This night, however, remained warm, but free of the humidity. The sun had not quite set and there was an afterglow of daylight that reflected off the clouds.

Anna hitched the horse to the surrey and Margaret took the reins. "Well, it's not the Cossack horde, but it will do." She snapped the reins. "Ya."

They rode out of town and into the forest. Soon, they climbed a road that wove between tall trees. Every so often they popped out of the woods for a moment to skirt the edge of the bluffs overlooking the sea. They rounded a bend and came to a turnout that faced east with the Atlantic Ocean spread before them. As they watched, the moon broke the horizon and climbed quickly to bathe the water and land with soft light.

In unison, they howled. Margaret poured sherry into the glasses and handed one to Anna. "Drink, Cossack sister." Anna sipped her sherry. Margaret downed hers in a single gulp, coughing and choking afterward. "Strong stuff on the steppes." She filled her glass and raised it to the huge, yellow moon. "To freedom." She drained the liquor and howled again.

The two women began laughing. Neither seemed capable of stopping. When one slowed down, the other looked at her, and the laughter started again.

Anna wiped a tear from the corner of her eye. "I have never done anything like this before."

Margaret took another drink. "We need to do more of it. Women are always told to be quiet and proper. Well, sometimes we just have to howl."

Throwing her head back, she howled long and loud. They started laughing again. Margaret went to pour another drink, but found the sherry bottle empty. A somber sense pressed down on her. "I just want to paint, Anna. It's what I was placed here on Earth to do. When I'm working on a painting, no matter how hard it is, no matter how much the subject fights me, when I'm working, I'm sane. I can't really attest to that at any other time in my life."

Anna had sipped only half of her original drink. "If that's true, dear, why don't you just paint?"

Margaret gave a short laugh. "John does not approve of my painting. Oh, ask him and he'll deny it. He's good at denying things. He'll tell you that of course I should paint, just not now. I have to draw the illustrations to sell more articles so we can amass enough money so we won't be destitute." She leaned over to Anna and whispered with a slight slur, "We are not destitute."

"Are you feeling all right, dear?"

Margaret shook her head slowly. "I haven't felt all right in years." She stared ahead blankly. "He wouldn't hold my hand, Anna. The baby was dead and he wouldn't hold my hand. I called him a bastard this morning. If he didn't hate me before, I guess he does now."

"I don't think John hates you. He must have been as crushed by the loss as you were, but men show grief differently. There has to be a reason he's grown cold. He's a good man."

Margaret slouched against the seat. "Oh, John is a saint. Ask anybody. He'll do anything for anyone, except me." She grabbed her head with her hands. "I loved him!" A wave of nausea ran through her.

Anna said, "Have you had a little too much to drink?"

Margaret's stomach went into convulsions. She jumped down from the surrey and vomited at the side of the road. It seemed the retching would never end. She felt Anna's cool hand against her forehead. When it did stop, she was drenched in sweat. "Oh, God, what you must think of me."

Anna retrieved a jug of water from the surrey. "I think you've held onto a lot for a very long time." She filled a metal cup and handed it to Margaret. "Here. Rinse your mouth, dear."

Margaret took a sip, swished it around and spat it out.

Anna said, "Now, do you feel better?"

Margaret was surprised to find that she did.

Anna said, "John is a reasonable man. Compromise."

"You can't compromise art, Anna." She walked shakily back to the surrey and leaned against one of the wheels. "He wasn't like this at first. He encouraged me to paint and helped me get my work into shows. That all changed when I lost the baby. I keep asking, 'Why? Did I do something?' But I didn't."

She closed her eyes. "I can't go on like this. I keep thinking about leaving him but divorce is impossible and even moving out could ruin my few chances of showing in a gallery. I could go back to New Jersey, but I'd have to explain it all to my family and I'd still be married to him and he'd have no obligation to support me."

"Those aren't the reasons, are they?"

Margaret wrapped her arms tightly around herself. "I still love him, damn it. I don't want to, but I do."

Anna put her arms around Margaret. "Be careful not to act in rashness or you might lose something that you can't get back. When the men of Glasen go out to fish, every wife knows that the kiss she sends him to the water with may be the last she ever knows. I was lucky with Alistair on Caribou Island. He always came back. But, I sometimes sent him off with some powerful curses, and if the sea had taken him, I would never have been able to live them down."

Margaret said, "How could we possibly reconcile now, after all that's happened?"

"Alistair and I had a lot of wounds to heal between us. We each forgave them, wiped them from our hearts, and never brought them up again."

Margaret shook her head. "It sounds too simple. Just forget the past?"

"Not forget, dear, forgive. Clear the slate and go on."

"But he'd have to change."

"Yes, he would, and so would you. But nothing can change if all you think abou' is how bad things once were and how you have to even the tally. Of course, if a man won't change or if he beats his wife, leaving may be the only choice. Is that John?"

They climbed back into the surrey. Anna took the reins and guided the horse back down the road.

The moon shone brightly, but under the shadow of the trees Margaret found it impossible to make out anything but the largest shapes. Even these took on a nightmarish quality. Darker clouds were gathering overhead. She silently hoped Anna knew the road well enough not to get them stuck.

The trees parted and allowed some moonlight in. Anna quickened the pace of the horse and Margaret felt a slight lift both at the welcome light and at the prospect of being back in Anna's house. What would she tell John and Alistair? Alistair would never believe the truth, though John might. She hoped he wouldn't ramble into a safety lecture. This gave her a little smile against the dark as she thought about what he would say if he knew half the things she had done in their travels.

The road turned inland as the trees drew close again. Anna pulled quickly on the reins and shouted, "Whoa." A tree had fallen across the road.

To the right there was a six foot high embankment. To the left was a soft shoulder that fell off into a ravine. The two women got out of the surrey and examined the fallen tree. Margaret tried to lift it, but it was too heavy. She inspected the shoulder to see if there was enough room to ride around without falling over the edge.

Anna said, "It's going to be a long walk back to the village. I don't know what Alistair will say."

"They're still smoking cigars and drinking brandy." Margaret walked along the edge of the road toward the fallen tree. She looked down into the ravine and saw that it was filled with thick woods. "Anna, if we could roll the tree into the ravine we could get by."

"Careful now. Maybe we should just walk home."

"And let John think I can't go out for a surrey ride? Let's…"

Her words were lost as the edge of the shoulder gave way under her foot and she tumbled over the side. She heard Anna crying out to her, but the words were lost in the wind that ran past her ears.

Branches crashed against her, starting as a light brush and cascading until she was enveloped in a sea of leaves and pine needles. She felt a sharp pain in her shoulder. Then, silent darkness overtook her.

The sound of a soft breeze came through the leaves and slowly grew in Margaret's ears, giving her the impression of ocean waves. At first she thought she was at the Jersey shore on a summer afternoon when everything was warm and calm and time had no meaning. She smiled as she breathed in and out. *That's good*, she thought to herself, though she had no idea why.

Slowly, she became aware of an earthy fragrance, rich with the smell of life. She knew she was lying on her back but didn't know how she had gotten there.

A sharp pain stabbed through her left arm and she opened her eyes. It was black. No light. No shadow. No cast of moonlight. No stars overhead. She waved her good hand in front of her eyes but could see nothing. "Oh God, no. Please, no. Not this. Not blind."

She tried to sit up. Pain erupted in her arm again. Slowly, Margaret flexed her elbow, then her wrist. The pain remained consistent but she could move her arm and so was certain it was not broken.

She felt around and found that she was lying on the forest floor atop a carpet of leaves and cool moss. Moving carefully to protect her injured arm, she got to her feet. There was no way of knowing where the road was or how far she had fallen. She felt numerous abrasions on her face and guessed the tree limbs had slowed her descent.

"Anna. Anna, can you hear me?" There was no answer. "Anna, are you there?" Panic nearly overwhelmed her. What if Anna had fallen, too? What if they were lost and no one knew where they were? It was such a foolish thing to do, all to spite John. Now she was lost in the woods. Worse, she was blind. Her art career was over.

"Oh God, no, no, no. Please no. Anna. Anna, where are you?" She shouted over and over. No reply came.

Her breathing slowed and the rational part of her mind took hold. Anna must have walked back to Glasen to get help. All Margaret had to do was stay where she was.

She heard a rustling to her right. "Anna, is that you? I can't see." There was no answer. Fear chilled her as she tried to remember if wolves or bears lived in these woods. She sniffed at the air and listened, motionless, as she searched for a clue as to what she had heard.

The snap of twigs came from behind and she felt a noose slip over her head. "So here ya' are, witch. Caught at last." The voice was unmistakably that of Beth Ramsey.

Before Margaret could react, her arms were pulled behind her back and a rope wrapped around her wrists. She screamed in horrid agony from her damaged shoulder. "What are you doing here?"

Beth Ramsey gave a dry chuckle. "Listening to your demonic cries up the road."

Margaret tried to free herself. Beth Ramsey gave the rope a jerk and the noose tightened. "Can't you see I'm hurt? I'm blind, for God's sake. I need help."

"I'll help ya', witch. Back to hell. You deny your demonic origins. Now, you can prove your claim. The river in this valley runs fast and deep. If you're a witch you'll float free of water. If not, I will know you are no witch."

Margaret followed the pull of the rope. Whenever she lagged behind, Beth Ramsey gave a jerk. They passed close to trees and bushes. Twice, Margaret stumbled and scraped her knees.

She began to see sparks flash before her eyes and slowly made out the glow of the lantern Beth Ramsey carried. The closeness of the trees gave way and a cool evening breeze brushed her face. Somewhere in the distance, an owl hooted.

Her eyesight was returning quickly, but everything was still a blur, even with the light of the full moon. The sound of a river running fast filtered through the trees. She tried to undo the bonds on her wrists. The pain in her shoulder was excruciating, but she continued to work the rope back and forth. It slowly loosened until she was able to slip one hand free. She pulled on the noose around her neck and threw it off.

Beth Ramsey was left holding the other end of the rope. "Then it is true. You are a witch."

A deep growl resounded nearby. Her eyesight had cleared enough to see that she and Beth Ramsey had stepped between a mother bear and her cubs.

The mother charged. Beth Ramsey screamed. Margaret said, "Get up into that maple tree. Hurry."

The two women ran with the bear in pursuit. A slight hint of rain sprinkled gently against Margaret's face. Beth Ramsey stumbled and fell. She covered her head with her hands. Margaret turned and pulled the rotund woman to her feet. "Come on. She'll kill you." Margaret put her arm around Beth Ramsey's waist and helped her reach the trunk of the tree. Beth Ramsey began to scramble up as Margaret pushed her. The bear was nearly on them. With a final shove she jumped, grabbed a limb, and climbed up.

The bear stood up on the trunk, its head a full six feet off the ground. It began climbing with its large, hook like claws. Margaret pushed on Beth Ramsey, hoping they could reach branches too slim to support the bear's weight.

It swiped and nearly caught Margaret's ankle. The cubs were now milling around the base of the tree and watching their mother. An errant thought ran through Margaret's mind. It was too bad she didn't have a sketch pad so she could take a pencil from her pocket and draw the scene below. "Idiot," she said to herself.

The rain fell heavier. It soaked the two women and the bears. The mother bear was moving up the tree. It was evident that the branches that supported Beth Ramsey and her would also support the advancing animal.

Margaret heard a slight pop, then another. A sharp, burning pinprick drove into her leg. As it did, she remembered the lye in her pocket from making soap with Sara earlier.

She pulled herself up higher into the tree with her good arm and gingerly reached into her pocket. The damp handkerchief burned the palms of her hand as she untied the knot. The bear lunged and she nearly dropped the handkerchief. She would only get one chance. With her legs wrapped firmly around a limb, she swung down and brought her face within a foot of the bear. The animal stopped and studied its adversary. Margaret opened the handkerchief and dropped the remaining lye directly on the mother bear's wet snout.

The bear shook its head, still staring at Margaret. An instant later it gave a great howl and dropped to the ground as the lye burned its face. It rubbed its nose on the ground and on the brush. The cubs gathered next to her and bleated in tiny voices. The bear turned and ran into the woods with the cubs behind.

The two women sat silently in the tree for some time. Margaret had faced death before at the hands of brigands and despots. In the end, an exchange of gold or bank notes ended the crisis. She had never known this raw, unrelenting fury of nature, and it left her shaken. The memory of the bear's hot breath inches from her face, well within reach of its paw, drove all thoughts of painting and John and Thomas from her mind. She started to shake. If she had not emptied her stomach earlier she was certain she would have vomited again. The shaking stopped but a rumble still echoed in her body. She looked to Beth Ramsey. "Are you hurt?"

"No."

"Do you think it's safe to climb down?"

"We should wait a little longer." The bombastic tone Beth Ramsey always spoke with was gone. Her voice was quiet, nearly a whisper. "No witch would have stopped to save me when I fell. I was wrong. I take back my words. But I warn you. The creature that lives with Ian is not human. Beware of her."

The sound of boots crunched through the underbrush. Margaret could see many lanterns approaching from different directions. The two women climbed down to the ground. John rounded a bend and stopped before them. A wide smile spread across his face. "Thank God. Are you all right?" He called back over his shoulder. "I found her. She's here."

Phillip Lamont appeared, followed by more men who filtered onto the path, each with a lantern in his hand.

Margaret said, "I landed hard from the fall and was temporarily blinded. Beth found me and helped me out of the forest. We were just heading back to Glasen."

Peter tilted his head. "Is that true, Beth?"

"Aye. I found Margaret in the woods and brought her out."

Peter looked to Margaret, and then to Beth Ramsey. "Well. That was fortunate."

John stepped toward her. "Anna couldn't see you from the road and we all thought the worst." Even by lantern light she could tell his face was ashen. "Oh God, the things that went through my mind." He reached out to take her hand.

She pulled away, her voice cold and distant. "I'm fine now, thank you."

She could not explain why she was acting so coldly or why she didn't tell him about Beth Ramsey's true plans or the bear.

John spoke quietly. "We were all just worried."

Phillip took Margaret's arm. "Let me help you."

She let out a cry of pain. Phillip let go. "You're hurt."

"It's nothing, really."

He called over his shoulder. "Where's Doctor Ferguson?"

"I'm right here."

A gray-haired man with a neatly-trimmed beard took Margaret's arm. "Well, let's just see. Where does it hurt?"

"In the shoulder. It really isn't that...ow!"

"Can you move your fingers?"

"Yes."

"Your elbow?"

"Yes."

"Can you move your shoulder at all?"

"Yes, but ...ow."

"Hmm. I don't think anything's broken. Probably a bad bruise." He examined Margaret's hand. "What's this from?"

"It's nothing. I was helping Sara make soap."

He took a jar of cream out of his bag. "Put this on your palms and wrap them in linen tonight. Come see me in the morning if you're still in pain. I think you need sleep right now more than anything else."

Phillip turned to the crowd. "Thank you, men. You've all put in a long night and, thank God, it has a good end. Let's go home now."

John floated through the men, shaking hands and thanking them for their help. They walked a half a mile to the road where several wagons waited. The men had chopped up the fallen tree and the party made its way back to Glasen. John thanked everyone once more before Phillip drove Margaret and John back to the Grants' house.

A fire blazed in the hearth. Ian sat in his chair and smoked his pipe. Sara sat next to him working a sampler. Ian looked up. "I hear there's been a bit of excitement."

"Margaret and Anna went for a ride and Margaret took a little tumble down a hill. I'm afraid I overreacted a bit and summoned the militia."

Ian motioned for them to sit down. "I wouldn't call a husband being concerned for his wife's safety overreacting."

Sara looked up from her needlepoint. "I'll bring some tea."

John said, "Please, don't bother."

Sara smiled politely. "It's no bother. Margaret can help me."

Margaret's shoulder was aching worse than before and she had no desire to leave the sofa, but before she realized what she was doing, she was following Sara into the kitchen. The fire in the stove had already been lit and a kettle came to boil. Sara put some herbs into a mug and poured hot water over them. "Drink this."

"Thank you, but I don't feel…"

"Drink." There was a command in Sara's voice that Margaret had never heard before. She sipped the hot concoction. It tasted as bad as another home remedy her grandmother had once given her. To her surprise, the pain in her shoulder and her palms lessened.

Sara said, "Now, why didn't you tell John about how Beth Ramsey planned to throw you in the river and about the bear?"

Margaret started to form an answer when she stopped, stared at Sara, and tried to comprehend how the young woman knew about what had happened.

Sara took a rock-like stance. "Don't bother to make up a lie. I've let the others go, but this time you could have been killed."

Margaret didn't know what to say. Gone was the impish Sara hopping around the room.

Sara returned the kettle on the stove. "You have turned an enemy into an ally. This says much about you, but Beth Ramsey is still unpredictable. You were very clever with the lye."

Margaret stared at Sara. "How can you possibly know anything about what happened tonight? I haven't said a thing to anyone. Did one of the men come by, or Beth Ramsey?"

"No one came here tonight. I know because it happened. Do you know why you didn't tell John?"

Margaret was tired and confused. "No. I just felt foolish because the whole surrey ride was just to get back at him, and then I got Anna stuck in the woods and nearly got myself killed."

Sara used a quilted pot holder to move the kettle off of the fire. "He was worried sick about you."

"I know, but somehow having him trying to comfort me just makes it worse." The old pain grew behind her right eye.

Sara poured hot water into a pot, put in a tea ball, and dampened down the fire in the stove. "He loves you, Margaret."

Margaret closed her eyes. "He loves his work and he loves himself. There's no room for anyone else."

"How can you say that?"

"Because it's true. He doesn't love me, Sara. He hates me. It's the only explanation for the way he's treated me for the last two years."

Sara's stern demeanor softened. "Do you look into his eyes?"

"What?"

"They're very sad, and very scared. Something about you terrified him, and he's afraid you will go away." She picked up the teapot and walked out of the kitchen.

The following week Margaret walked into the village to sketch the shops she and John had first passed when they entered Glasen. She did not need any more drawings, but she wanted to distract herself from Thomas and Blossom. Her arm had been badly bruised in the fall, but after another draft of Sara's concoction the pain vanished along with all traces of the lye burns.

Autumn had arrived in full glory and the morning dawned cold and foggy. She wore her long coat and a woolen cap, remarking to herself on the dramatic change from just a few weeks before.

She began with the butcher shop. Anna Lamont pulled up in her surrey. Kathleen Myers sat next to her. Margaret said, "Hello Kathleen. How are you feeling?"

"Not so good today, ma'am."

"Please, call me Margaret. What's wrong?"

"Maybe I'm just tired." She patted her swollen belly. "He's been keeping me up nights with his kicking."

It was the first time Margaret had heard Kathleen refer to her pregnancy. She said, "So, you've settled on a boy."

"Oh, it just has to be ma'am, I mean, Margaret. James wants a son so bad."

Even though the doctors and nurses never told Margaret the gender of her baby, she too had been certain. For her, the child she carried in her womb was a girl. She smiled. "I'm sure you're right."

Anna said, "I'm driving Kathleen out to the sawmill James's late uncle used to own."

"Has your mother-in-law sold it yet?"

"She sure wanted to," said Kathleen, "But Fr. Williams had a talk with her and James's aunt. They made a deal where we'll work the mill and they'll get a share of the profits. I thought with all the bickering this would never come to pass, but as my mother used to always say '*Cha do dhùin doras nack d'fhosgail doras*', and I guess she was right."

Anna said, "And this is one of the best opening of another door that I've seen in a long time."

The exact translation of the Gaelic proverb eluded Margaret, but the gist of it seemed clear enough. "This is marvelous. When are you moving in?"

"As soon as James gets back from this voyage with Mr. Drummond. He's giving up the sea for good and I'm so relieved. Every time he's out I'm just scared they'll hit one of those big storms and he won't come back."

Anna pointed to two open crates in the rear bench. "Kathleen wants to take some things out so they can move in as soon as James lands. Would you like to come along?"

Margaret had intended to finish sketching the shops before supper, but the chance to draw a sawmill sounded intriguing. "All right. I'd love to."

She climbed into the surrey and squeezed in next to a trunk. "Will we be back by supper?"

"Oh, by lunch, I should think. Hopefully this will be a quieter trip than the last one."

Margaret blushed and sat silently.

The ride started pleasantly, though foggy and cold. The fog soon lightened to reveal the fall colors were at their best. Bright, vibrant yellows, oranges, deep reds, all splattered like paint shot from tubes. They passed a point where the limbs of the trees arched overhead, nearly forming a tunnel. A burst of wind shot through the branches, catching leaves and spraying them across the road like a multicolored snow flurry. The leaves twisted and twirled in small spirals and settled on the ground, only to be picked up to dance once more on the breeze. She wished she had brought an easel and oils to capture it all.

They traveled southwest past the Grants' house. A few miles later they took a fork to the right that wound back into a forested area of spruce, pine, birch, aspen and maple. Around a bend they came to a river that had been dammed. Just below stood the mill. Most of the water poured over a flood gate, but a sizable torrent was diverted through a slough and over a huge wheel that turned rapidly. The road ran up to a cabin that overlooked the mill pond.

No one was around. Anna pulled up to the cabin. Margaret helped Kathleen get down from the surrey and supported her by one arm. Anna said, "Let's unload these crates and be gone. You don't look any too good, dear."

Kathleen bit her lower lip. "I feel fine."

Anna lifted the crates from the rear bench and placed them on the ground. Kathleen took two steps toward the cabin, then screamed and leaned into Margaret.

Anna grabbed Kathleen's other arm. "What is it, dear?"

"I don't know. It was a sharp pain." She cried out again. "Something's wet between my legs."

Margaret checked beneath Kathleen's skirt. Her bloomers were soaked. "Your water's broken."

Kathleen put her hand over her mouth, "Something's pushing inside me."

Anna took Kathleen's arm. "Quickly, let's get you back in the surrey and down to Dr. Ferguson."

Margaret said, "There's no time. The baby's coming now. Help me get her inside."

They supported Kathleen's weight and guided her into the cabin. There was no furniture, only a stove next to a sink and some cabinets.

The young woman breathed rapidly. "Oh God, I'm scared."

Margaret held her hand. "Your baby boy is going to be here very soon now. Anna, help me get her bloomers off."

Kathleen's belly rippled with a contraction as she cried out again. "Mother Mary, save me."

Anna took Margaret aside. "Have you ever delivered a baby?"

"No. Have you?"

"No. The doctor gave me ether for mine, so I don't even know what they did."

"Well, I still remember my labor and I was with my brother's wife when my niece arrived. I also watched the birth in that African village."

"But you only watched."

"It will have to do." She handed Anna her handkerchief. "Get a pail or pot of water from the pond and wet this as a cold compress."

"What are you going to do?"

"Keep Kathleen from panicking."

Anna left the cabin. Kathleen fingered the beads of her rosary and prayed. Another contraction came that was closer than the last.

Anna returned with the wet handkerchief and dabbed Kathleen's forehead.

Kathleen grimaced in pain. "I have to lie down. Something's wrong. I know it."

Margaret held the young woman's hand. "Anna and I are here."

Another contraction came. Kathleen was in tears. "Oh Jesus, help me."

Margaret was immersed in images of her own labor and her dead child. "Your baby will be fine, but you have to do exactly as I say. Do you trust me?"

Kathleen nodded her head.

"All right. Anna. I saw some clean sheets, a knife, some twine in the crates. There's a bucket next to the stove. Put some water to boil so we can sterilize everything."

Kathleen covered her belly with her hand. "You're not gonna cut my baby out?"

Margaret stroked the young woman's hair. "Of course not. The knife is to cut the umbilical cord."

Anna returned. "I've got some water on the stove and everything's set to be boiled."

Margaret said, "We have to keep Kathleen walking."

Anna looked at Margaret. "Lord, she's in labor. Put her on the floor."

"No. She has to walk around, let gravity pull on the child."

"I think we should get the doctor."

Margaret whispered in Anna's ear, "He'll never make it in time. I need your help. I won't let this baby die."

They helped Kathleen walk across the floor. Anna said, "How do you feel, dear?"

"The pain's not as bad, but I don't know how much longer I can stand up."

"It won't be long," said Margaret. "Here. Lean against the wall for a minute."

Kathleen rested, then walked across the floor again. Anna went to the kitchen and returned with the sterilized sheets and knife. Twenty minutes later, Kathleen put her hand on her belly. "Something's moving."

Margaret raised Kathleen's skirt. "The baby's coming." She spread the sheet on the floor. "Kathleen, you need to squat down here. Anna, put your hands under her arms and support her from behind."

Kathleen squatted as Anna held her under the arms. A tiny head crowned. "Kathleen, the baby's coming. Be ready."

The next contraction came. Margaret shouted, "Push."

Another contraction. Another push. The shoulders were clear. In an instant, the baby shot from the birth canal and slid into Margaret's arms. Blood was everywhere, spattering Kathleen's skirts, soaking into the sheet, covering Margaret. "It's a boy, Kathleen. You have a son." The newborn began to cry.

Margaret cut and tied off the umbilical cord. "Take her outside. She can lie down in the rear bench of the surrey while we wait for the after-birth. Bring one of the clean sheets." Margaret held the newborn. It was amazing to see this fresh life, a complete human in miniature down to the tiny, fully formed fingernails.

Anna guided Kathleen to the surrey and tossed the sterilized sheet across the rear bench before helping the young woman in. She then covered Kathleen with a lap blanked. The new mother gave a laugh. "I thought it would really hurt, but it all just happened."

Margaret placed the newborn in Kathleen's arms. A broad smile radiated from the young woman's face. She opened her blouse and positioned the baby boy's mouth over a nipple. He continued to cry. Then Anna leaned down, stroked his cheek, and he started to suckle. She smiled. "Well, I know a couple of tricks." All three women laughed.

Kathleen cradled her baby, stoking his head and talking to him in coos.

Anna took Margaret's arm. "I'm sorry I doubted you."

Margaret patted Anna's hand. "We defied the wisdom of western medicine today."

Anna nodded. "How do you feel?"

Margaret looked to the new mother and child. "Whole, as I haven't felt in years. I wanted to have a funeral, but they cremated my baby before I woke up. They called her 'it' and told me I should just forget the whole incident. I was forbidden to give her a name."

"Did you?"

"Yes." Margaret wiped her face with her sleeve. "Her name was Sara, and now I know she is finally at peace."

CHAPTER ELEVEN

The day of the ceilidh dawned bright and cool. In one respect, Margaret was interested in seeing the celebration as she had watched so many around the world. At the same time, she wanted to be left alone by everyone, especially John.

She climbed up to the loft and prepared materials for Thomas's lesson that afternoon. A creaking sound came from below. She was about to shout for Thomas to come up when the main doors of the carriage house opened and flooded the interior with a near-blinding light.

She crouched down and peered between two crates to the floor below, hoping that whoever had opened the door would not spot the easel she had just set up. More, she prayed that Thomas would see the large doors standing open and stay away.

As her eyes adjusted, she saw that it was Ian. He walked slowly forward and placed his hand on a fender of the carriage. Margaret fought to slow her breathing. Ian bowed his head and mumbled something she could not hear. He looked around as if he were searching. She prepared words in her mind to explain her presence, knowing that nothing she could say would appease him.

His gaze swept across the floor. He walked over and lifted a small wooden box. With it secured under one arm, he mounted the carriage and sat on the rear bench. He opened the box and took out a photograph, followed by another. From Margaret's vantage point it was hard to make out details, but she could discern general shapes of buildings and people.

He held up one of a man, a woman, and an infant. Margaret remembered the photographs she had found when she first explored the carriage house. Ian ran a finger over the picture. He stopped and looked up to the double doors. Sara stood at the threshold, her form silhouetted against the outside light. Ian returned his attention to the picture. "They called to me."

"It was an echo in the fog, Ian. They are at rest."

"They said it was cold and the kelp was tangled about their feet." He held the photograph close to his chest. "They won't let me go."

Sara climbed the carriage, gently prodded his hands away from his chest and held them to her cheek. "Lizzie and Samuel are beyond all cares of this world. No one could have saved them, not even you."

"Sometimes it's not enough for a man to be merely who he is."

She kissed his hand. "Oh, Ian. Who else could have a hold on someone like me? You know I cannot leave you. No mere man could do that."

A partial smile lit his face. "I sometimes wonder how it is that you came to me."

She smiled back. "Because you are kind and gentle and strong of heart. Now, come inside. I'll make some tea. Tonight we'll go to the ceilidh and dance with our friends till dawn."

Ian nodded his head. "I'd like that." He stood up and looked around. "Is Margaret here? I don't want her to see me like this."

"She's not in the house."

Ian got down and placed the box of photographs on the floor. Sara took his arm. "We'll take the carriage out tonight and let its spirit breathe. That will ease the calling."

"We shall do as you say, my love."

Sara started to close the doors, then stopped. "Ian, do you like them?"

"Who?"

"Margaret and John."

"As odd as they are, I think I do, but I'm not certain they like each other."

Sara thought for a moment. "Their hearts say they do, but they're too confused and proud to admit it. It's very sad."

The doors closed. Margaret sat silently in the loft as the voices of Ian and Sara discussing her love life rang in her head. She banged her fist against the floor boards. "Damn you. Damn all of you."

By the time Thomas arrived, Ian had returned to sea and Sara had gone walking off to the village for some buttons. Margaret critiqued Thomas's portrait of her, pointing out his strengths of composition and weaknesses in technique. The lesson lasted half an hour and Thomas focused his attention on every word. Margaret used paper from a sketchbook to demonstrate some different effects she wanted Thomas to practice. When she was done she pulled a crate over. "Well, I guess you'd better get started right away." She began to unbutton her blouse.

He said, "Wait. Please. I just want to do your face today. Come sit close to me."

"All right." She pulled the crate closer and sat down. He studied her intently for several minutes before painting.

She kept her gaze slightly to the right. Still, she could not avoid his eyes when he examined her for long minutes at a time. It felt deeply intimate, almost intimidating.

He worked silently. She lost track of just how long she sat. He put his palette and brush down and walked up to her. He came closer. Her heart beat hard up into her throat. He brought his face to within an inch of hers and slowly moved his gaze over her skin. She felt his breath on her cheek. He reached out and stroked her lips with a fingertip. A tingle danced down her arms and across her back as her eyes involuntarily closed. She wanted to scream. She wanted to run. She wanted to take him in her arms and press her lips against his.

Thomas nodded his head and returned to the canvas. Margaret played out a scenario of Thomas holding her, stroking her, giving her the affection she craved.

He painted for fifteen minutes. "I'm through for the day."

Margaret sat for a moment longer, the images fading slowly from her mind. She stood shakily and walked around to study Thomas's work. She found the portrait disturbing. The eyebrows dipped slightly to form a protective hood over the eyes that were tinged with a ragged line of red around the edges. The mouth was a thin slit with lips slightly blue.

"Is that what you saw, Thomas? That much longing and hurt?"

"Not at first. Not until I came over and studied you. Then I saw it. That's why I touched you."

Her ears started to ring. A feeling she could not identify formed in her chest like a lump. "You could have told me what you wanted. I would have posed."

"It wouldn't be real then. I had to see your true feelings come up. How else could I paint them?"

When she had posed unclothed for her classmates it was aloof and sterile. They were only painting her body. Thomas had exposed her more than if she had walked naked down the street. She had trusted him and now felt betrayed. It took all her will not to slap him. The throbbing pain behind her right eye was nearly blinding. "How dare you use me like that. You could have told me what you were doing. I'm your teacher."

"I was just trying to do what you taught me."

"I never taught you to use people."

"I was only…" He paused and sat the brush down. "This will never work. I can't go on being close to you and far from you. I can't come back."

Margaret shook her head. "You have to come back. You can't stop now. We can change things."

"What use is it? What use is anything? I can't have you. You'll always be tied to John. I've been nothing more than a distraction. We both know that. I love you, Margaret, but I now know that you will never love me. Please don't try to speak to me again." He walked quickly down the stairs and out of the carriage house.

Margaret sat motionless for several minutes. She felt nothing in particular, thought of nothing specific. She walked over to Thomas's painting and clinically examined the scared and lonely woman he had caught. From a technical standpoint she had to admit that his method for getting the emotion out of her had worked. No amount of coaching could elicit that look. She remembered a lecture by Robert Henri.

> *"Look to the emotion that is there in the subject and find how best to express it through your art."*
> *Margaret had raised her hand. "But how do you know when you've crossed from expressing the subject's emotions to injecting your own?*
> *"Ultimately, everything in the painting is your own emotion. That's all you can really know. What you must strive for is the authenticity of your subject, because that will draw the authentic emotions from within yourself."*

She raised the canvas covering Blossom's portrait and remembered how she had provoked the woman into revealing her emotions. She asked herself how she could fault Thomas for doing the same thing she had done. Then, she asked herself how she had made such a mess of her life.

"Ceilidh. Ceilidh." Sara jumped and clapped her hands together. "It's going to be so exciting. We'll dance and eat and sing."

Ian smiled as he pulled on the jacket of a fine black suit. "But first, we have to get there, and get there in style we will. I have a surprise."

Margaret knew what the surprise was, but dared not reveal it.

A knock came at the front door. Ian opened it to reveal Phillip Lamont standing on the porch in a silk top hat and tails. He removed the hat as he stepped inside. "They're ready to go, Ian. Sven says you can return them to pasture whenever you're done."

Margaret leaned out the door and saw that there were two horses in full bridle and harness tied to the rear of Phillip's wagon.

"Could you help me with the horses, Mr. Talbot? You ladies just wait here." Margaret had broken down the easels and hidden everything behind crates, but a rush of fear still washed over her as she hoped no one climb up to the loft.

As the men walked out and closed the door, Sara slipped her hands around Margaret's arm. "There's magic in the air. It'll be a fine ceilidh."

A few minutes later, Ian opened the front door. "Ladies, your carriage awaits."

Outside, the fine, black carriage, now pulled by two chestnut mares, stood ready. The gold trim gleamed in the light of the lamps. John, in a borrowed beaver pelt top hat, stood by the open carriage door like a footman. Ian extended his arm to Margaret. She took it gracefully and climbed up to the padded leather seat.

John escorted Sara, who giggled the whole time. With the ladies seated, he and Ian mounted the driver's bench. He gave the reins a snap and they rode off toward Glasen.

Sara's bonnet was exquisite. Made of pink silk, it had eight rows of hemstitching, two rosettes, and a wide tie. She edged conspiratorially close to Margaret. "It's Japanese silk. Ian paid two dollars and fifty cents for it. Can you believe that?" She put her hand over her mouth. "Oh. Am I bragging?"

"Yes, and that's perfectly acceptable."

Margaret wore her wide brim hat with the chiffon lace. It was fast falling out of style, but it traveled well.

She leaned over to Sara. "Your husband is certainly in a festive mood tonight. What did you do to him?"

Sara stared blankly at Margaret for a moment. Suddenly a smile of recognition came to her face. "Oh. You mean, did I do something to make him happy? It wasn't me. Not really. I just remind him of who he is, and he makes himself happy."

Margaret settled into the ride through the air of a crisp autumn evening. Stars shone brightly against a black sky, their steady lights blocked momentarily as clouds floated slowly by, only to be blazingly revealed moments later as the clouds passed.

When they reached the village, every head turned to stare at the magnificent carriage and the picture of Ian driving it down the road. People pointed and shouted, "Wonderful!", "Take her in, Ian!", and "The squire has arrived."

The dance was held in the brick warehouse on the wharf. As they approached, Margaret heard music rolling over the water. It was filled with the steady thump of drums, the resonance of fiddles, and the reed-rich sound of pipes.

Ian pulled the carriage up in front of the warehouse. John opened the door and Ian escorted the ladies to the ground. "I'll tie up the horses. Wait for me here and we'll make a grand entrance." He climbed up on the driver's bench and snapped the reins again.

As he drove off, Sara hopped from one foot to another. "Just look at all the people. This is going to be so much fun. Let's all dance together as soon as we get in." She gave a squeal. "Look. Anna and Alistair. I simply have to talk with them. They can dance with us." She ran off to the Lamont's surrey.

Margaret and John stood silently, each staring in different directions. She heard John give his nervous laugh which meant he wanted to say something. He looked slightly past her. "Margaret, we should try to enjoy ourselves tonight."

"What makes you think I don't intend to?"

He clasped his hands behind his back and looked down at his feet. "I know things aren't going right. I know they haven't been right for a while. I'm very sorry about it, and I wish it wasn't so."

Margaret began to ask why he didn't do something about it if he felt sorry, but caught herself. "A truce for tonight?"

"I guess that will have to do, even though…"

"Please, John. I can't think past tonight."

He gave a sigh. "All right."

Sara returned with Anna and Alistair in tow. Anna fanned herself. "Lord, but the fire of this child wears me out just watching her sometimes."

Alistair shook John's hand. "I'm glad you're here. I was afraid you might not come."

John said, "How could we miss it?"

Ian arrived. "Well, shall we all go in?"

The warehouse was filled with people talking, eating, sitting, drinking, dancing, and singing. The younger people all gathered together at one end. A gentleman would bow to a lady, who would then curtsy and extend her arm to be escorted to the dance floor, all under the watchful eyes of several chaperones.

The musicians consisted of six men. Two were fiddlers. Two more played handheld drums called *bodhrans* that looked like large tambourines without bells. Another played a Scottish wire string harp called a *clarsach* and the sixth, a set of bellow pipes that gave a soft, dreamy sound.

They played lively jigs and reels and the slower strathspeys. At the beginning of each song, people lined up on the dance floor, either in two rows facing each other or in a square.

"Come on," said Sara. "They're starting again. Let's all dance."

Margaret saw John begin to protest, but he abandoned it when Sara took his hand and dragged him to the floor.

Eight partners lined up across from each other, alternating man, woman, man, woman down the line. John stood across from Sara, and Margaret was opposite Ian.

A fast jig began. The couple farthest from the musicians came to the center, locked their left arms together and, with their right hands held over head, spun twice counter-clockwise. Then, they locked their right arms, raised their left arms, and spun twice clockwise. The man took the woman by the arm and escorted her to the next gentleman in line. He and the woman repeated the dance of linking arms and spinning. The first man took the woman's arm and escorted her to the next man. This continued until the woman had danced with every man in the two lines. There was quite a bit of winking and flirting.

The first couple then spun twice in both directions and the woman now escorted the man to dance with every woman. When it was Margaret's time to dance she grinned and giggled as she spun around. Giving an audible "woo", her head became light, which only made her laugh harder. She had no idea if she was doing things right or wrong, and she didn't care.

When the head man had danced with every woman, the couple then held hands and danced down the center toward the musicians, released hands and joined the line at the end. The new head couple then linked arms and started the dance again. The music stopped before Margaret and Ian could become the head couple and she never had the chance to dance with John.

Margaret leaned on Ian, who helped her back to a set of kitchen chairs set along the walls. Sara, John, and Anna joined them. Alistair appeared a moment later with two glasses of punch and handed one to Anna.

Margaret fanned herself with her hand. "That punch looks good. I think I'll get some."

John stood up. "I'll get it for you. Just rest."

She looked at him. "Thank you."

Ian took Sara's hand. "Would you like some punch, my dear?"

"Oh, yes. Please. And some of Flora Brown's shortbread."

Ian squeezed her hand and got up.

Margaret scanned the warehouse as a low rumble of voices echoed off the walls. "Has anyone seen Thomas Brown?"

Alistair looked around. "I don't think so."

"He's probably helping his mother," said Anna.

John returned with two glasses of punch. She took it carefully, avoiding any contact with his hands as she looked up at him. "Thank you."

"It is my pleasure."

A squeal of delight from Sara heralded Ian's return with punch and shortbread. "This is so good. She makes the best."

Margaret swirled the punch in her glass. "How is Flora? I haven't spoken to her in a while."

"She's fine," said Ian.

"Was Thomas looking well?"

"Can't say. He wasn't over there."

She silently sipped her drink. A familiar voice said, "May we join you?" She looked up to see Angus Sinclair standing next to her with the urn containing Mary's ashes under his arm.

Sara clapped her hands. "Mr. Sinclair. Mary. I looked for you."

"We came a little late, my dear. Mary just couldn't decide what to wear, so we went through her closet together trying on gown after gown. But, as always, she chose just the right thing."

"You look lovely, Mary," said Anna.

"The picture of beauty," said Ian.

Sinclair gave a chuckle. "Oh, look. You've made her blush."

Another dance was forming. Sara stood up and clapped her hands. "Let's all dance again. It was so much fun."

"I think I'll sit this one out," said Margaret. "I'm still a bit warm. Perhaps I'll take a walk outside."

John got up. "I'll join you."

"Oh, no," said Sara. "I'm not losing two of you at the same time." She whisked John off before he could offer a defense.

The music started. Sinclair sat down and tapped his foot as he watched the dancers.

Two men walked up in front of the musicians and began dancing. Their arms and bodies were held rigid as they moved their legs in a pattern of four steps on the right foot followed by the same four steps on the left. The pattern was repeated several times until a new one was introduced.

Sinclair looked to Margaret. "They're clogging. I was quite good at it once."

Margaret said, "Are you and Mary going to dance, Mr. Sinclair?"

Sinclair smiled broadly. "Mary and I just like to sit and watch the young folk now."

Three lines of dancers formed on the floor. The couple at the head held hands and danced in a sliding motion up the center and back down to the head again.

"He's worried abou' you," said Sinclair.

Margaret turned to him. "I beg your pardon?"

"Mr. Talbot. You were sick, weren't you?"

She hesitated. "Yes. A few years ago."

"He's been worried abou' you ever since."

"It would be nice if he showed it."

He held the urn close to him. "We all show things strangely sometimes. There was a time when I'd forgotten to tell Mary how much I loved her. Do you remember, dear? I would be cross when I didn't mean it. It hurt you, didn't it? But, I still loved you. You see, Mrs. Talbot, Mary has the greatest capacity for love and always forgives me. Now I go nowhere without her, for she is my life."

Margaret sat silently, not knowing what to say. Her lip quivered and she wasn't certain if she felt a sudden pity for Sinclair's madness or sadness for the love she herself had lost. "You're a wonderful man, Mr. Sinclair." She looked to the urn. "I'm envious of you, Mary."

"You don't need to be. Your husband loves you very much. I can see it in his eyes, and in yours. Don't act too late." He stood up. "We promised to find Phillip. If you will excuse us." He walked off across the floor with the urn tucked tenderly beneath his arm.

Margaret walked outside and down to the end of the wharf. The sounds of the party reverberated off the water in an echo that was pushed back by a stiff breeze coming in from the ocean where clouds were gathering.

It felt good to be alone with the sea. She reached the end of the wharf. Crates had been stacked there to make room in the warehouse for the celebration. She walked around a tall box and came face to face with Thomas.

He took a step back. "What are you doing out here?"

Margaret forced a smile. "I didn't see you at the dance."

"That's because I wasn't there."

Silence enveloped them. Margaret listened to the lap of waves against the pier as a breeze picked up. "Everyone was asking for you."

Thomas looked out over the water. "Don't lie again. No one ever asks for me."

"What about your own lie? I know you're angry. You think I led you on after you exposed yourself." She stopped to rub her forehead. "Thomas, I only wanted to teach you to paint. I don't know how everything else happened, but I am so sorry."

He turned slowly toward her. "Who the hell are you to treat me like some puppy you hit with your carriage? You don't realize what you've done, do you? I had some kind of life here. I knew I'd spend the rest of my days scraping boats and making pictures that no one would care about. I knew I'd never find love. I knew I'd always have the shame of being what I am, but at least I was blissfully ignorant of what I didn't have.

"Then, you came. You wanted to make me into a great artist, but I'm not your great artist. I'm just a fool who draws pictures. I can never have any of the things you showed me, including love. You can't possibly be sorry enough for that."

Margaret's face heated as she grabbed him by the shoulders and shook him. "Hate me if you want. Curse me and blame me for everything, because it *is* my fault and I should be dammed for it. I can take your hatred. I deserve it. But I cannot suffer the thought of you abandoning painting and never knowing the artist you can become. I can't live with that shame. Yes, shame, Thomas. I know what it is. I bluster and position and push people around, but underneath I'm scared most of the time and ashamed the rest. So stop feeling sorry for yourself and blaming all your troubles on epilepsy, or Glasen, or me, and do something about it."

He closed his eyes and shook his head. "I can't hate you, no matter what happens." He opened his eyes and looked into her hers. "I know I can't have you. I always knew. It just felt so was wonderful."

She said, "Let's go into the dance."

A slow strathspey was playing as Margaret and Thomas walked into the warehouse. Flora Brown, both hands grasping a sheet of shortbread, stopped, looked at Thomas, then at Margaret. Margaret smiled. Flora narrowed her gaze and walked away.

Margaret forced her smile to remain as she nodded to other people. "Come over and see everyone else."

"I'd rather not."

"Please. It would make them happy."

"Them or you?"

"Please."

Thomas followed Margaret over to the chairs with his hands in his pockets. "Look who I found," she said.

John looked up. "Hello, Thomas. Have you made any drawings lately?"

"I'm working on one now. I call it betrayal."

John raised an eyebrow. "A heavy subject."

"Don't be dour," said Sara as she came over and pulled Thomas's hands from his pockets. "This is a dance, not a wake, though I haven't quite gotten the difference yet."

Ian indicated a chair next to him. "Sit down, lad. Would you like some punch?"

"No, thank you." Thomas took the seat and started to put his hands back in his pockets, but stopped when Sara cleared her throat and frowned.

The music stopped. A voice with a decidedly Midwestern accent bellowed across the floor. "Talbot. There you are. Just the man I wanted to see." Jonah T. Underwood was swaggering directly for them. Morag followed with a doting gaze upon her face. Underwood wore a black suit with white tie, gloves and tails. Morag was adorned in a floral pattern ball gown with three layers of silk lace, each more delicate than the one below. Ruffled lace formed a modest 'V' neck with silk rosettes on the shoulders. Opera gloves covered her hands and arms and she held an oriental fan that she opened and closed, but never actually used. Her coiffure was adorned with a tiara.

Ian rolled his eyes toward the ceiling and shook his head. Underwood showed no notice as he ignored everyone but John. "I think you will find this most illuminating, Talbot. Now, what would you say is the most delicate problem at any party?"

"Boors?" said Ian.

"Plates," said Underwood. "There are never enough, and they all have to be washed afterward. Not much fun for the hostess, wouldn't you say, Mrs. Talbot?"

Margaret pursed her lips. "As Ian says, boorish." Ian looked over to Margaret, the corner of his lips raised slightly.

Underwood said, "So-called inventors, such as Edison, produce absurd products with no practical use to the modern woman who is trying to keep a home, wouldn't you agree, Mrs. Talbot?"

Margaret was amused to find herself fighting to control laughter instead of rage. "Do go on, Mr. Underwood."

"Indeed. At a party like this there are many different foods to partake of, and most, by nature, tend to break apart into small particles. We, in the scientific community, refer to this as being 'crumbly'."

The inventor cast his gaze around the group. "I can see that each of you has been captured by the prospect of this problem, and you are all wondering 'What has Underwood come up with?' Well, this." He pointed to his tie. Margaret now saw a white roll of fabric that blended into Underwood's shirt. He extended his gloved hand, palm up, and Morag placed one of Flora Brown's shortbread cookies in it. "Observe." He raised the shortbread to his mouth. As he did, the roll unfurled, forming a six-inch square of material directly beneath his chin. He took a bite and a few crumbs fell onto the square. "If I had spilled those crumbs on the floor, I would have executed a grave social faux pas. However, my new 'Snap-O-Bib' has saved me any embarrassment." He popped the rest of the shortbread into his mouth and lowered his arm. As he did, the Snap-O-Bib rolled back up, trapping the crumbs inside.

"Though a series of wires and rods, it is activated automatically with the mere movement of my arm. What do you think of that, Talbot?"

John cleared his throat and looked the device over. "Well, I have to admit that I've never seen anything like it before."

"I plan to go into production next month, just a trial run, mind you. No more than a thousand. I'll mount an advertising campaign, of course, but I need the world humming about the 'Snap-O-Bib'. That's where you come in, my friend. I'd like you to take a dozen with you and give them to your fellow journalists. When they are seen wearing them at parties and begin writing about them, well, I think you can see where that could lead to."

John nodded his head slowly, "Oh, I could see where this was leading quite a while ago."

"Good. Well, the next set's starting. Can't contain that old Scottish blood pumping through my veins. We'll be in contact."

Angus Sinclair walked across the floor with Mary's urn still under his arm. "Has anyone seen Phillip? I can't find him."

No one could recall where Phillip was. "Well, thank you," said Sinclair before he walked off.

"Pity," said Underwood.

"What do you mean?" said Margaret.

"That poor wretch living in delusion. I've read of cures that could help shock him back to reality."

Margaret said, "Just what do you think he needs to be shocked out of?"

"Well, look at him."

"I *have* looked at him, and I find him to be one of the wisest, one of the most compassionate, and one of the sanest men I have ever met."

"Ms. Talbot, I hardly see such qualities in Mr. Sinclair."

Margaret stared into his eyes. "No, Mr. Underwood. I don't believe you would."

Underwood raised an eyebrow and headed for the dance floor, followed by Morag. She turned suddenly and ran back, a look of awe on her face. "He's a genius." She scampered after her husband.

Ian sat back and sipped some punch. "He's a loony." Everyone, including Thomas, burst into laughter.

The musicians played another reel. Three sets of lines danced with lively steps. At the end of the set, one of the fiddlers stood up and tucked his instrument under his arm. "We will now play a waltz. Gentlemen, if you will escort your partners to the dance floor, we will begin."

John stood up and extended a gloved hand to Margaret. She looked up at him. Her first thought was to ask just what he wanted. Everyone was watching her. She looked to Sara who was oddly quiet. John held his hand steady. Margaret stood slowly and reached out to take it.

The musicians readied their instruments. John put his hand on her back and held her close to him. It had been many years since they had waltzed. The thought of embarrassing herself surfaced for a moment. The music began, and Margaret pressed into John's body as she fell into the dance with practiced ease. They stared into each other's eyes, never wavering. Margaret's pulse quickened. He had taken her hand before in Glasen, but why would he want to touch her now, or even speak to her after her outburst at the Grants' house? He wanted something, that was evident, but she could not imagine what it was.

Should she say something? Ask about the weather or the article, perhaps? No words came. She had intended to remain aloof and distant as they danced to get it over with. Instead, the habit of all their years together filled her with longing for the life they once had. She closed her eyes and leaned her head on his chest, listening to the pounding of his heart.

Her grandmother had told her so many times about magic spells to hold a husband close. She wished there were such a thing to capture the instant in a glass bottle and hold it unchanged, forever.

The music ended. The other couples left the floor. John held Margaret tightly. "Margaret, I…" He pursed his lips. "I need to say some things to you. I've been…" Again, he halted. She reached up and brushed her hand gently against his cheek. He took her hand in his. "When you lost the baby. When you almost died, the doctors said… I never wanted to hurt you. I wanted to be with you, but after what they told me I was just so afraid that…I would lose you."

"How? Did you think I would leave you? I wanted you near me, John. I needed you near me."

"I know. It tore me apart, but they said…"

The door of the warehouse blew open. Margaret turned to see that the breeze from before had grown into a full storm. Phillip stood in the doorway. "It's the *Lion*. She's going down outside the harbor. I need men for the rescue boat."

Margaret and John ran back to the others. Ian stood up. "Hugh Drummond's schooner is sinking offshore. We have to send the rescue boat out or everyone on board will drown for sure."

John said, "I'll go with you."

Margaret took him by the arm. "Let them go, John. They know what they're doing."

"She's right, Mr. Talbot. It's dangerous work to say the least."

"I'm a strong rower."

"John, let Ian go."

"Margaret, I have to. They'll die."

"This isn't a game."

Phillip said, "I need two more. Ian?"

"I'm with you."

"Anyone else."

John shook off Margaret's hand. "I'll go, Mr. Lamont."

Phillip looked him over for a second. "All right. Let's go."

Margaret grabbed John again. "Anyone else here can do this. Don't you see? You could prevent someone from being rescued."

"They need me."

"What about me, John? You were about to tell me something on the dance floor. I've been waiting two years to hear you say it."

"People will die. I have to help."

"When do I get your time? When are you going to talk to me?"

"I'll be back."

She shoved him away. "Go on. Leave. That's what you're best at. Why don't you just drown yourself out there?"

He stared at her before turning and walking out of the warehouse. Margaret stood still, wondering what to do. She ran out the door. The wind slapped cold rain into her face and drove it up her nose. Lanterns cast a dim illumination and she could only make out the silhouette of a long rowboat being taken from a building and placed in the water. Men climbed in, ten of them, eight rowers, Phillip on the tiller and Ian in the bow behind a small cannon. Phillip shouted, "Oars in. Take us out, lads!

Pull!"

Margaret ran forward. Anna's tale of fishermen kissing their wives goodbye and never returning filled her mind "John. Wait. Please." She reached the edge of the wharf as the boat moved slowly through rolling white caps. Against the crash of water and wind she could barely make out Phillip's voice continuing to shout, "Pull!"

She looked down at the churning sea beneath her feet. "Oh, God. Don't let him die."

She felt someone take her by the arm and pull her back from the edge. Thomas's voice said, "What are you doing? You could drown if you fell in."

They stood there together for a moment. Thomas let his arm slip around her waist. She did not protest.

A loud boom resounded off the water. Lanterns were lit on the rescue boat and she could see a puff of smoke from the cannon. In the feeble light she could just make out the mass of the schooner.

Thomas peered into the darkness. "They've shot a line into the rigging of the *Lion*. They'll take the men off one by one."

"How many men can they rescue at a time?"

"In these seas, not more than six before heading back to the wharf. They'll have to make three trips at least."

The oarsmen held the rowboat away from the schooner while a life preserver was hauled up the line to the deck of the floundering ship. Sewn into the hole of the life preserver was a pair of pants with the legs cut short. A man on the *Scarlet Lion* got into the pants and was lowered to the rowboat that bobbed like a toy on the surface of the ocean. Six men were taken off and the rowboat returned to the wharf. As soon as the survivors came ashore, they were engulfed in the arms of wives and mothers.

The rescue boat was off again. Another cannon blast secured a line in the rigging and six more men came off. Margaret rubbed her eyes from the strain. The ship was noticeably lower in the water. "How much longer will she stay afloat?"

"Not long. Pray they have time for one more trip."

"Won't the rescue boat sink too?"

"She has sealed air pockets built into her hull for buoyancy and baffles that let water flow out, but block it from getting back in."

The boat returned and released its human cargo. Margaret noticed Fr. Williams standing next to Kathleen, who cradled her newborn son in her arms. "Thomas, is James Myers on that schooner?"

He turned around and looked toward Fr. Williams and Kathleen. "Aye."

The rowboat headed out again. As it reached the mouth of the harbor, an immense wave rose up like a bluff before it. The boat seemed to loom, suspended in space, before crashing down into the sea. She could see only swirling water with no sign of the boat.

Thomas said, "Phillip and Ian are with him. Hold your faith."

Like a bubble bursting to the surface, the rowboat shot from the water, all hands safe. Margaret fell to her knees.

With a third cannon blast, the grappling hook flew for the rigging but missed. A fourth shot missed as well. Thomas stood at the edge of the wharf. "They only carry six charges." Margaret could plainly see that the schooner would never stay afloat long enough for the rescuers to return from shore again.

The cannon fired. The grappling hook caught in the rigging. One man came down followed by another. As the third man was lowered, the rigging gave way. The line went slack and the life preserver fell into the churning water. The rope was pulled taut, but when the life preserver broke the surface, it was empty.

A wave slammed the rowboat against the hull of the schooner. The men pulled on their oars. The rescue boat backed off. Something bobbed to the surface next to them. Two rescuers pulled the man who had fallen from the life preserver into the rowboat.

One man remained standing on the deck of the Schooner. "That'll be Hugh Drummond," said Thomas. "The captain's always the last to leave."

Drummond stood at the railing. The schooner gave a shudder, which nearly knocked him down. Ian prepared to load the cannon again. Drummond waved them off, stood on the edge of the railing, and dove in.

Once he hit the water, the *Scarlet Lion* made a groaning sound and rolled over on her side. She bobbed on the surface for just a minute and sank beneath the waves.

The oarsmen pulled hard to escape the sinking ship. A rower leaned over the side and pulled Drummond from the sea.

The rowboat returned to the wharf among cheers from the onlookers. As soon as it docked, men leaped to the waiting arms of family and friends. Lastly, Phillip and Ian carried a body ashore and laid it on the wharf. Margaret looked down at the lifeless face of James Myers.

Kathleen pushed forward, her baby held tightly in her arms. The villagers fell silent. Kathleen stared down at James, her mouth taut, her head shaking slowly. A scream exploded from her throat. Kathleen fell on the body, still holding the infant as she pulled at James's hair and stroked his cheek. The baby cried in her arms. His tiny voice was overshadowed by his mother's wails.

No one came near. No one spoke. When Kathleen's sobs grew barely audible, Flora Brown laid her hand on Kathleen's shoulders and helped the young woman to her feet. Gently, she guided Kathleen and her child to a circle of women who stood off and apart from the rest of the villagers. Some were old and some young. The circle opened and allowed Kathleen to enter before closing in around her.

Thomas said, "The widows of Glasen. They'll take care of her now." He looked at Margaret. "This is how my father died." He turned and walked away.

The rain slowed. Margaret looked for John. He and Ian coiled rope near the boat. She ran to him.

He looked up blankly. A second later he went back to coiling rope.

Ian lit his pipe. "You did well out there, Mr. Talbot. I'll be frank. I didn't think you had it in you."

"Thank you. Neither did I."

"Would you care to take my second dory out and fish with me tomorrow?"

"I would like that very much, sir."

CHAPTER TWELVE

Margaret was awakened by a deep-throated cry the next morning. Pulled from a dream, she thought at first that she was standing back on the wharf and hearing Kathleen Myers. But this sound came from behind the house. John was not in bed. She threw on a dressing gown and ran outside.

The doors to the carriage house were wide open. John, Ian, and Sara stood before them. In Ian's hand was the portrait of Blossom.

John looked up at Margaret with a blank expression. No one spoke. She tried to form words, but knew it was too late for excuses. John entered the carriage house and climbed the stairs to the loft. She could see him holding up Thomas' portrait of her. He climbed back down without a word.

Ian looked tired. His hands shook as he held the canvas. Margaret expected him to destroy it. Instead, he set it gently against the open door of the carriage house. "Mr. Talbot, we should be fishing."

John nodded his head.

"You'll need to dress proper," said Ian. "Slick, sou'wester, boots.

I've extras inside." Ian, John and Sara walked past Margaret and into the house.

Margaret wasn't certain how long she stood there in the chill morning dew wearing only her dressing gown. With a shuffling motion, she retrieved Blossom's portrait and climbed to the loft.

She propped it up against a crate, moved Thomas's work next to it and studied them together, the eyes, the stance, the arms. In both portraits she saw the same resignation, the same loss of control, the same sadness. There was no strength, no determination, none of the things she had wanted to express. Margaret had intended to make a statement about a woman who overcame adversity. All she saw was her own failure.

A lecture by Robert Henri came back to her.

> *"The artist is in everything he paints, beauty, ugliness, joy, despair, nobility, debauchery. All this comes from within the artist. The model acts as a mirror, a catalyst for the painter to expose himself and thus express his own views and opinions."*

She shook her head. "What kind of artist am I? I can't even accomplish what I taught Thomas." She told herself she would never be an artist because there was nothing inside of her to say. All the years now seemed a sham. "It's true. I *am* just a lousy hack."

With a deep growl, she grabbed the scraping knife and drove it into Blossom's portrait. Again and again she assaulted the canvas with slashing cuts. She sliced at the arms that refused to show strength. She stabbed at the head. She gashed the throat. She gouged out the eyes that mocked her own weakness. Grabbing a tube, she splattered red paint across the canvas. "Die, damn you." She hurled the tube to the floor and looked up. Sara stood before her. Margaret absently fixed a loose strand of hair on her head.

Sara walked around and looked at Thomas's painting. "Where I come from, we have a name for the look on this face." She made a high-pitched screech. "You would call it the weeping sickness, where you're out of place and don't know how to get back. I feel it when I watch the ocean." Sara looked to Margaret. All her childlike qualities were gone. "The difference between us is that you are not just lost, you are unaware that you are lost. I know how to get back, but I will not leave as long as Ian lives. All that I was and all that I know calls to me, but I have made my choice, for to be with Ian is to be home."

As soon as Sara said the word *home*, Margaret knew beyond all doubt that it was that sense and feeling that she had sought all her life, and only now recognized. She had had it once with John, though she never put that word to it. Now, she desperately wanted it back.

Sara moved to the mutilated painting and smiled. It was not the innocent sprite smile, but one of understanding. "Yes. Thomas was right. This is a portrait of you, not Blossom. You have found it at last."

"Found what?"

"Your passion."

"What are you talking about? It's destroyed."

Sara said, "Yes," and climbed down the stairs.

Margaret packed her clothes. How could she could slip away by herself? The last thing she wanted was to stand before Ian again. She tried to tell herself that she had done what she had to in order to paint. "Who are you trying to fool?" She threw the dressing gown into the back of the trunk she had once used to secrete the painting. "You've only managed to make a fool of yourself." Using both hands, she crushed her hat into another trunk. "You were going to make such a noble statement. What an idiot. You have nothing to say and no voice to say it with. Just give the whole thing up and go." But go where? She thought of New York, then New Jersey. Wherever she went, she was certain John would not follow.

Just weeks before, she had wanted to leave him and paint. She desperately wanted to know what it was he had almost said to her at the dance. It had felt so good at that moment, like home. She slammed her fist into the trunk. "I was so close!"

One of the shutters came loose and slapped against the house.

Margaret looked out the window. The sky was darker than twilight, though it was not yet noon. She pictured John in a small boat on a stormy ocean. A crash came from Ian and Sara's room. Margaret called, "Sara, what happened?" There was no answer. She pounded on their door. "Sara, can you her me?"

She threw the door open. A tree limb was sticking through a broken window. Glass and wood were strewn everywhere. The force had scattering Sara's treasured collection of sea shells and driftwood across the floor. A cold wind drove rain through the shattered pane. Outside, a flash of lighting struck a tree and sheared off the top.

Margaret went downstairs. "Sara?" No answer came. She ran through the back door. "Sara!" Her voice was blown back by the force of the storm. Drenched after just a few steps, she fought her way down to the dock where Sara stood with her shawl over her head.

She turned at Margaret's approach. "For five years I have watched the sea each time Ian went out. It has always wanted him, but I have not allowed it. Today, after we talked in the loft, I remembered the sea and forgot about the storm. The ocean saw."

Margaret grabbed Sara by the shoulders. "Stop talking nonsense. You're always talking nonsense. I don't know what's the matter with you, but this is the real world, that storm is real, and John's out in it." It was over between them, but she couldn't stop caring, though she didn't know why.

Sara said, "Oh, Margaret, you know very well why you care."

Margaret started to explain when she realized she had only thought the words and not spoken them aloud. A tingle started in her spine and radiated out. She felt an urgency to run somewhere, anywhere, but she couldn't make her legs move.

Sara pulled on her shawl. "You understand much that you hide from yourself. When you first came, I thought it was a game. I've never really understood your games, except for cards."

It took all of Margaret's strength to speak. "What are you?"

Sara turned back to the sea and made gibberish sounds as she had when she stood naked at the well. A thin line appeared in the clouds that allowed a sliver of sun to shine through. As quickly as it had emerged, the line snapped shut. Sara lowered her head. "It is up to Ian, now."

There was a simple explanation for all this. Margaret was upset. The eerie feeling came from the lightning charges. She just had to get a hold of herself. Her voice became calm and rational. "Will they be able to reach the dock?"

"Ian will beach the dories. The storm would smash them against the dock."

The rain made it hard for Margaret to see more than a few dozen feet ahead. "If they're coming in to the beach, shouldn't we be there?"

"I cannot touch the sea."

Margaret could understand Sara's fear of being swept out by the waves that smashed into the gravel shore. "We can stand back near the bluff. That should be safe enough."

"I cannot touch the sea."

"When the boats come in they'll need our help. Don't you care about Ian?"

Sara turned and studied Margaret. "You cannot imagine what he means to me. That is why I cannot touch the sea."

"Well, I'm going down there." Margaret started for a set of steps that led down to the coarse gravel.

Sara shouted, "Wait." After a long silence she said, "I'll come with you."

They stood against the face of the bluff that gave them some small shelter from the wind. The rain, however, continued to pour. Margaret considered going back to the house for a rain slicker but she was already soaked and might miss John's return.

Margaret pointed to a gray shadow that bobbed on the water before her. "Sara, look."

From the ocean a dory beat its way slowly to shore. Margaret started forward. Sara yelled, "Wait, or you'll be swept out."

A single boat was driven into the beach by a large wave. Ian jumped out and hauled the dory away from the water. Sara took three steps forward and stopped. Margaret ran on. Ian slumped against the hull, his breath labored.

He looked to the bluffs where Sara waited and ran up the beach to envelop her in his great arms. She leaned into him and wrapped her own arms around his body. He said, "You shouldn't have come so close to the water."

"The sea mocked me, and I was so afraid for you."

Margaret looked into the boat. It was empty. She ran to the cliffs. "Where's John?"

Ian spoke between breaths. "Don't worry. Your husband's in the other dory." He pointed to a rope tied to a cleat. "He was too inexperienced to row further, so I've been towing him. Help me haul in the line."

He and Margaret took hold of the rope and pulled. It seemed far too easy. The next second, all tension left the line and its frayed end emerged from the water. John's dory was nowhere in sight. Margaret put her hand over her mouth. "Oh, God."

Ian said, "I know where that dory has to be. I'll go back out and get him."

Sara shook her head. "The sea will keep you if you go."

He took her hands in his and held them tight. "I watched my Lizzie and Samuel drown. I couldn't save them, but I can save John Talbot. I will not have another death on my conscience. It would be too great a thing to bear."

She placed his hands on her cheeks. "No, Ian. Please."

He put his finger to his lips. "Shh. Don't be afraid."

An acrid smell cut through the air as the blinding flash of a lightning bolt struck the dory, blasting it apart and setting the wood on fire.

The rain extinguished the burning shards that hissed and smoked. Margaret should have become hysterical. Nothing came to her, not even a sense of emptiness.

She gazed out to sea for John in the same way Sara had watched for Ian. That pose had struck her from the moment she first saw Sara Grant. Now, she was the one waiting, but, unlike Ian, John would not return.

She looked up to Sara standing next to the old fisherman who now seemed tired and broken. Once more, Margaret could not look away.

The scene dimmed except for Sara, who shone brightly against the background as she had when Margaret first saw her so many weeks before. Margaret's throat tightened once again. This time she did not faint. She stood still on the beach, though she no longer noticed the gravel or the rain. The nonsense song her grandmother sang to her as a child played in her ears. This time she remembered the last phrase. *The balance is two drops of blood and we must choose the path.*

She struggled to make sense of it. All she could think of was Sara. "The balance point," she whispered to herself.

Every encounter Margaret had ever had with Sara, every image, every sound, flashed through her mind. It had been comforting to believe that the young woman suffered from hysteria. It placed her strangeness in the realm of rational science. Hysteria could explain why she never touched the sea, why she did not know common customs, and what spurred her to stand naked by a well while singing in a babble.

But, it didn't explain why Margaret had known what the babble meant, or why she was drawn into the image it conjured, nor was it hysteria when Sara knew what Thomas had said about Blossom's portrait, or how she knew Blossom's name when Margaret had told no one, not even Thomas.

A sense of panic rose in Margaret as she had never known before. Every fact about both her grandmother and Sara felt like an avalanche descending. A thought came to her that was completely absurd and defied every rational fact, yet she could only draw only one conclusion. She stumbled across the coarse gravel beach and grabbed Sara by the arm. "It's true. You *are* a selkie. Save him, please."

Ian pulled Sara close to him. She patted his hand and turned to Margaret. "I will not leave while Ian lives."

"John will die." She shook Sara by the arm and began to drag her toward the ocean.

The young woman who seemed so frail grabbed Margaret by her rain-soaked blouse and lifted her off the ground with one hand, leaving her feet dangled above the pebbles. "I will not touch the water yet." Sara tossed Margaret across the beach as if she were a doll. Margaret began to stand but a sharp pain in her leg forced her to one knee.

Sara walked across the beach and stood before Margaret. Her voice took on a reprimanding tone as though she were speaking to a willful child. "You have made me hurt you. That is against my nature and very painful to me. I will not leave Ian for anyone else's life. I have one chance to walk the earth and love as you do. Would you have me forsake that?"

"He'll drown."

"Last night you told him to drown himself. Is this not what you want?"

The memory of her own words stabbed into her. There were no lies she could tell to change things. Fate had granted her what she asked for, and, powerless, she hated herself for it.

She knelt in the gravel and tried to think of an argument to convince Sara. The sound of the surf droned through the rain. Again, she thought of her grandmother and a time when she was playing on the other side of sand dune and her mother came storming across the beach with her jaw set tight.

> *"Don't sing these songs to her. She's not going to make that choice."*
> *"You and I have rejected the balance of blood. She must choose her own path."*
> *"Not Margaret. I'll send her as far away from the sea as I can. I won't lose her the way we did Aunt Gloria."*

Margaret had not understood the conversation as a child. Kneeling in the gravel in front of Sara the memory became deep and dark. She managed to stumble to her feet. "What does the blood mean? It can save John, I'm certain of it. Tell me."

Sara said, "You already know. You've known from the moment you first saw me on the bluff. You felt the balance tilting and you were afraid."

"Just tell me. Stop making everything into a puzzle."

"I cannot tell you what you already know. You wouldn't hear it. You always look for reasons outside yourself and never listen to your heart."

Margaret started to argue but stopped. She asked herself what it was that seemed to bind her to Sara and immediately thought of water. Water flowing in sinks and at wells. Joyous songs of the sea that were gibberish to all ears but hers. She closed her eyes and thought about the vision as she asked herself how she had felt when she had heard Sara's songs. She had felt like a seal rushing through the water. An even greater terror pressed through her skin that was worse than before. She opened her eyes. "I'm a selkie, too!"

Sara looked out to sea. "Since time forgotten, selkie maidens have taken human husbands and when the sea called the selkies back, the children were left on shore. The blood of fairy has passed through the female line of these selkie children from grandmother to mother to daughter, and so it has come to you. But you cannot return to the ocean, as I will one day. You were born on the shore, and in your veins flows one drop more of human blood than fairy. This binds you to the land, though you will always know a longing for the sea."

Margaret stared at the ocean as rain poured down her face. "Then there is nothing I can do. John is lost." Though she said it, she could not accept it. There had to be an answer. "Sara, what did my grandmother mean by balance of blood and a path?"

"You do not want to know."

"Can it save him?"

Sara turned away. "If a human of selkie descent receives two drops of blood from a true selkie, the balance shifts from human to fairy."

"Would that make me a true selkie?"

"Yes."

Margaret stared into the gale. "Please, give me two drops of your blood."

Sara turned back around. "You do not know what you ask for."

"I would be like you. I could save him."

"Once chosen, the path is set. A selkie maiden may take human form but once in all her existence. When she touches the sea again, she returns to her fairy form forever. Never has a selkie returned to human form a second time."

"I can stay away from the ocean after rescuing John."

Sara shook her head. "You have had your time in human form. I can give you two drops of my blood and you can then rescue your husband, but you will leave this world, everything you have known, all that you have loved, all that you have been, your friends, your home, your art, even the husband you save, never to return to those things."

A moment before it had seemed a simple choice. Even if she didn't love John, she didn't wish him dead. But, she didn't know if she could give up everything and never paint again.

It would be so easy to walk away and simply not act. If she could just hate him, vilify him, see him as a monster, she could let him drown without guilt. There wouldn't even be the shame of divorce. He was lost at sea. No one would ever believe a selkie offered her a way to save him.

She thought about the death of her baby and the way John had abandoned her emotionally and refused to touch her. She recalled how he forbade her to paint and how he would only talk to her about the articles. All the anger and pain rose to the surface as she pictured a man who had betrayed her. With these images in mind, she asked herself how she felt about John and stopped to listen to her heart. A single word came to her. *Home*.

It shocked her. How could she still love him and see him as home after all that had happened? She tried with all her will to hate him. She could not.

The first time she had realized she was in love with him was when she had just returned to a boarding house in New York while he was still on an assignment. She had felt giddy and silly, and she had liked it. Sitting in her room, she had crossed her arms over her chest and imagined it was his arms wrapped around her.

Margaret stared at the ocean. "He'll die if I don't save him."

"The sea will take him in Ian's place, and the waves will bury him."

There was no lecture from Robert Henri to fall back on. Logic defied her. Even her anger was drained. Her eyes fixed on the dark waters. She extended her hand. "Give me your blood."

Sara took a fish hook in one hand and Margaret's finger in the other. She thought of running and had to fight for just enough courage to stand still. The hook gashed a short incision. She winced and concentrated on the pain, not wanting to think any further ahead.

Sara pricked her own finger and held it over Margaret's wound. Two drops of blood fell into the cut. "It is done."

Margaret studied her finger. "That's all?"

"What did you expect? Stage magic? The balance is tipped. You are a true selkie."

Margaret started to argue when the cut on her finger healed as though the incision had never been made. Something else was different. Neither the wind nor the rain felt cold anymore.

Sara kissed Margaret on the cheeks and made the screeching noises. This time, the sounds clearly said, "Hurry, sister. You can only help him in human form and you will not remain so for long."

Margaret said, "How do I swim if I am not a seal?"

"You will never be a seal. You are a selkie. You swim because it is what you do. Shed your human clothes, they will only slow you. Go now."

She stripped naked and leaped into the surf.

At once, she was enveloped in ecstasy. The water rushing passed her skin filled her with such joy that she sang a song.

> *Dive deep,*
> *Beneath the ocean waves,*
> *The water rushing by;*
> *Embrace the everlasting thrill,*
> *For we shall never die.*

There was no need for air. She felt no fear. At first she tried to swim with her hands and feet, but soon discovered that she moved by her own will far more easily than using any swimming movement. Her arms trailing at her side, she looped and turned, playing with the water. She could imagine herself being nowhere else. What foolishness it was to walk on the land and be limited by paths and feet when all the sea was open and free.

She swam farther from shore. The lure of the ocean called her to go even farther and seek out the selkie communities where she could play games. Memory of the human world faded rapidly. There was only the sea and the waves and rapture beyond measure. She thought, *I'm home.*

The word gave her pause. She could barely recall having been human, but she did remember she had entered the sea to find home. But not a place. A feeling. A person.

John.

The human Margaret emerged. She had to save John. Rising to the surface, her new senses reached out across the ocean until she found a single dory adrift in the storm.

The ocean called her again. "Come and play, forever play," she heard it say, and knew the sorrow Sara bore. She felt a physical pull to swim away and forget all human existence. Yet she wanted to save John and bring him safely to shore. The weeping sadness held her for an instant before she set off for the dory.

She sped now with human purpose. There could not be much time left to her before she took on selkie form, even if John was still alive. The hull of the dory came into view. She shot from the water into the boat.

The dory was half filled with rain. Margaret pressed her hands together and cast them apart. The water flew from the boat and into the sea. John lay unmoving, his head against the gunwale. She reached out and laid her hand on his forehead.

Though the storm-churned waves shook the boat, her body remained solid in the dory. She held John's head to her breasts and sang a song whose words would have been nonsense in John's ears had he been conscious. Margaret did not fully comprehend why she sang, but she knew it was right.

John stirred and spit up water. His head lobbed back and forth but he did not open his eyes. As she probed his mind and sang the healing song, she saw his thoughts as if they were her own.

John sat in a paneled doctor's office. Diplomas and books lined the walls. The doctor wore a three-piece suit as he sat behind a mahogany desk.

"Please, Mr. Talbot. Take a seat."

John settled into a padded chair directly across from the doctor. "When can Margaret come home, Dr. Keen?"

"That depends on her recovery, of body and mind. She has suffered a great trauma. She nearly died."

"Yes, Dr. Dexter told me, and I am grateful for everything everyone has done. But both Margaret I will want to plan the funeral of our child."

Keen sat back in his chair. "There can be no funeral. Stillbirths are disposed of in a medical fashion, but in any case, your wife must forget the infant as soon as possible. She is in danger of succumbing to hysteria, which would require further treatment."

"Are you saying Margaret is insane?"

"No. But she is in peril of losing control of herself. Such women have been known to take their own lives. You can never mention the baby. Take her on a trip somewhere. You may even need to change homes. Her mind must be taken off of the incident until she can get over it. Some women take longer than others."

John rubbed his forehead. "Of course. I'll do anything for Margaret. We'll go away for a month, six months. I'll tend to her every moment and hold her tightly."

Dr. Keen leaned forward, his hands clasped before him, his elbows on the desk. "No, Mr. Talbot. You cannot hold her. Should your wife ever again conceive it would certainly kill her. Your resolve may be strong, but you are a man with a man's needs. If you must, find release in other ways. Any intimate contact could lead to her death, and the most innocent contact can lead to intimacy. You cannot touch your wife, even to take her hand."

John said, "I've just lost my baby! Do you want me to lose my wife as well?"

"I am saying you will lose her to death as you did the child if you do not follow my directions. Although women are naturally prone to hysteria, many recover once they accept reason."

John stared blankly at Dr. Keen, then put his face in his hands and cried.

The memory faded in Margaret's mind. Other incidents from John's life after the stillbirth came to her; John moving into another bedroom and crying behind the door, his constant struggle to obey the doctor, his desire to keep them together by forcing her to draw the illustrations, the fear that she would leave him if her paintings made her a success, the twist of his gut while he wrote the poem she had found. Each incident was seen with a detached air, as if she was watching a play. At the same time, she felt every emotion and pain John had experienced as if they had happened to her.

John opened his eyes as his body shivered. He looked around shakily with confusion in his eyes. "Margaret? What are you doing here?"

She smiled. "I've come to take you back."

John shook his head. "You can't be here. I'm dead and this is my damnation."

She held him close to her naked body and gently rocked him. "You are not damned. You are loved."

She recalled incidents from their life together. They were not the larger moments such as their wedding, the travels to exotic places, or the awards they had won. They were the little things she remembered just then; a time they paddled a canoe on a lake, their first kiss, a dinner of no particular significance, looking for a set of cufflinks that he was already wearing and laughing themselves silly. For an instant, the world vanished, except for her and John, and she knew to her bones and her soul that she loved him and that for her, he was home.

She wasn't certain if she could forgive two years of pain in an instant. If they were going to be together, there would be many things to work out. Then she remembered that they were not going to be together. These were the last moments she would spend with him. She asked herself what could possibly matter but the moment. Tears mixed with sea spray stung her eyes. She placed her arms tightly around him as the dory was tossed from side to side.

The storm gained strength. She stood and surveyed the horizon. From her throat came a sweet, melodic call. It surprised her, and she wasn't quite certain what it meant. A moment later, the sea around the little boat began to churn. The sound of barking filled the air. All about the boat, hundreds of seals bobbed on the water's surface. The boat gave a shudder, and Margaret looked down to see a carpet of seals lift the dory on their backs and carry it toward shore.

The boat reached the gravel-strewn coast. The seals pushed the dory up onto the beach. As if in resignation, the storm ended. Margaret lifted John and laid him on the rocky shore. He coughed, half sat up and looked around.

With John safe, the call of the sea pulled at her. She stepped back from him. "I have to go, John. I can't come back."

"No, Margaret, don't go. For the love of God, don't leave now."

She wanted to tell him that the weeping sickness was too great, but no words came.

John lurched forward and fell to the gravel. "Margaret. Stay. I've been a coward and a fool. Abandon me, I deserve no less, but do not abandon your destiny as an artist. I could not bear that."

She stepped back and nearly tripped. Looking down, she found that her left foot had become a flipper. In amazement, her hands transformed as well. She tried to speak, but only garbled sounds emerged. A wave ran up her body, like having a tight nightshirt pulled off. Her nose grew long and pointed, her hair became fur, her body tube-like. She fell to the beach in seal form.

John's voice came from behind but the call of the sea was too great. With a leap, she dove into the waves and once more bliss enveloped her.

She raced and swam and skirted the bottom. There was no past or present, only the instant where experience melted behind her and she went forward.

A selkie voice nearby said, "Let's play chase."

She rushed onward to find four other selkies swimming in a tight knot, rubbing against each other, spinning and diving, breaking out to have the others follow before forming back into a close ball.

They stopped and stared at her. "Come play," one said. Margaret charged in. She had no idea what the game was, but as it began, she instinctively moved and matched the other selkies. Their touch sent ripples of pleasure through her body more intense than any lovemaking. When she broke out to be chased, thrilling excitement flooded her. When she was caught and brought back to the ball, which she allowed herself to be, she felt whole and complete, giving all of herself and receiving all of the others.

In her human life she had never trusted anyone or anything completely, not even John. Always, she held a small part of herself back for fear of being consumed and losing her identity. For the first time in her life, she abandoned all restraint without fear or condition.

Margaret never wanted to stop. "I could do this till I die."

"Silly," said one. "You are new from the human form. You have forgotten. Death is only for mortals."

This took a moment to be absorbed. Then, the concept became obvious, like something she had just forgotten.

She wished John were there to share the joy with her and remembered that he would never be there again.

His face appeared in her mind. She remembered his eyes and his smile and wondered if he would learn to forget her. She had hurt him. She had hurt many people. Her temper had spoken cruelly, especially to those she had loved.

Would anyone remember her art? Blossom was to be her masterpiece, a statement about strong women overcoming adversity, yet she wasn't even able to overcome her own failure as an artist. Certainly the world would be better off without her.

The game stopped. The other selkies gathered around her. One of them said, "You think of what you left behind. This will pass. Soon the human world will be but a dream of a dream. You will feel their weeping sickness no more."

Beneath the waves of the Atlantic Ocean, Margaret heard, in her mind, the last words Robert Henri ever spoke to her.

> *"Do not imitate me, Margaret. Eclipse me. Find your own style, your own passion. It is likely that a hundred years from now no one will know my name. That doesn't matter. I shall live on through you and through those you teach and those they teach. We are the shamans, we artists, retelling stories as ancient as humanity, set for the time we live in. Do not look to me, or anyone else, for approval. Only you will know when you have achieved greatness."*

The other selkies waited for her to act. She went to the bottom of the ocean. There, she arranged some rocks and shells onto two, intertwining circles. She removed some stones from one of the circles, leaving it broken.

The three selkies swam around the display. They smelled it and brushed it. One of them said, "What is this?"

"Art," said Margaret.

They inspected it for a moment longer before another selkie said, "Let's play racing." They shot off into the sea, leaving Margaret alone.

She thought about the ruined portrait of Blossom after she had ripped it with the knife. It expressed exactly how she felt at that moment, all of the emotions, all of the fears, all of the despair. It was the passion inside her; the passion she had always looked for and missed because she was waiting and hoping for someone else to tell her that she was an artist. She stared at the two circles on the sea floor. "I do what an artist does, because I am an artist, because I say so."

She turned around and swam as fast as possible back to shore. All the time, Sara's warning about never being able to return to human form bounced inside her head. She forced it away, thinking over and over in her mind, *I am an artist. I will be with John. I will live in both worlds.*

She had no idea how long it had been since she entered the sea. In selkie form time had no meaning. She might have been gone an hour, a day, or a year. The beach came into view. She stuck her head above the water. Ian was helping John up the steps as Sara followed.

Margaret pulled herself onto the beach. She said, "John, come back." All that came out of her mouth was a garbled sound that bounced off of the bluff face. Ian turned around. Sara stood silent. John stumbling down to the beach toward Margaret and fell to the gravel.

Margaret and John crawled toward each other and touched hand to flipper as they met. An ecstasy more fulfilling than the selkie game glowed inside her. It seemed oddly humorous that she should feel so close to John only after changing into a blubbery seal. Here she was, a human transformed into a magical creature contemplating what it was like to be human. The absurd image made her laugh, which sounded like high-pitched whistles. John started laughing as if he understood the joke.

They rolled on the gravel beach making high-pitched squeals and deep-throated laughs. He took her in his arms and stroked her pelt. The years in which he had withdrawn his affection floated up within her. The pain of abandonment returned with all the intensity it had held and festered. She remembered Anna Lamont's words. *Forgive.* Each stroke brushed away a little of the pain, but there was so much left.

The longing for the ocean returned and she heard the *ceol-mara*, the music of the sea. Her eyes, no longer human, surveyed the world of mortals around her. She could not stay there. She struggled free of John, her selkie strength far out matching his human powers, and headed again for the water. Like a faint echo, his voice called her back, but they could not match the *gait na mara*, the laughter of the waves.

As she was about to touch the water, John's voice cut through that of the ocean's. "Sara. Give me your blood. Let me become a selkie, too, so I can go with her."

Margaret halted. She knew from the nuances of his tone, the subtleties she had learned to interpret so well over the years, that he fully realized what he offered. In an almost detached sense it surprised her. She never thought he would give up his articles, his notoriety, his parties, all for her. It wouldn't work, of course. He had no selkie blood in him. Still, the offer of his sacrifice filled her with a longing the sea could not match, the desire to be with him.

Her selkie body tried to enter the water, but her humanity held firm to the land. She thought of her art, her travels, and her life with John. A garbled, yet human voice screeched from her throat. "I will stay."

Pain beyond anything she had ever imagined ripped and twisted and tore at her body. Her screams filled the air. Every muscle cramped in torment. She thought her skull would split. All the pain of her stillbirth magnified a thousand times exploded through bone and sinew. John's arms were around her as he held her close to him.

Something snapped and she was certain her back was broken. A voice inside wished for death to come and relieve the pain, but she shouted in a croaking hiss, "I am human. I am an artist."

She looked at her flippers. Out of them arms appeared, then hands and fingers. Spasms contorted her stomach and she vomited up seawater in violent spews.

She was cold and wet and remembered that selkies felt neither. She reached down and ran her hand over herself. The seal form was gone. Shivering, she lay naked in her human body.

John took off his coat and placed it around her. Sara touched Margaret and jumped away as though she had touched some wild beast.

John looked to Sara and laughed. "Don't be so surprised. There is no other like Margaret."

His words came sweet and gentle to her ears. The clouds parted and warm sunlight bathed them. She studied John. His face was familiar, yet seemed fresh and new. Everything around her was new and bright. Streams of vapor rose from the sun-drenched gravel. Each unique wisp fascinated her. She looked to the sky, to the bluff and out to sea. As she listened, there was a quiet yet persistent call. "Come play."

She turned to John. He still held her tightly, his face tense and lined. She said, "You're afraid I'll leave again."

He started to speak and began to cry.

She smiled and snuggled into him. "Silly. I'm home now."

The going away party at Phillip Lamont's house flowed out into the street as people from all over Glasen came to see the Talbots off. James Duncan was more than happy to delay the journey and helped himself to pies and cakes and shortbread and not just a *wee dram* of scotch.

"Now, you be certain to write us when you get safely home, dear," said Anna.

Alistair shook John's hand. "We'll be waiting to see the article, Mr. Talbot."

"Yes," said Fr. Williams. "I imagine you've found plenty of contrast between New York and Glasen."

John looked to Margaret, then back to Fr. Williams. "I'm not certain about that. Both places are filled with people who are noble and base and courageous and cowardly, but who, for the most part, care about their families and their neighbors and try to do the right thing. The article won't be quite what I set out to write, nor what my editor expects, but I think it will be far better. Perhaps changing centuries isn't quite as important as I thought."

Margaret noticed someone standing off to the side. She approached and found Beth Ramsey standing between two buildings. The older woman said, "I hope you will not think unkindly of Glasen because of me. Few show me kindness."

"I will remember Glasen fondly. I only ask that you show kindness to yourself and others. It will be reciprocated."

Beth Ramsey turned and walked away.

Margaret made her way through the congratulating crowd to Ian and

Sara. "It is very hard to leave now. My life is just happening and I have so much to learn."

Ian said, "I hope you can forgive a gruff old man. You've helped me lay my past to rest." He took Sara's hand. "None of us knows how long we have with someone else. It's best to remember what's important, and what's not."

Margaret touched Sara's cheek. "Thank you, sister. You will always be with me."

Sara touched Margaret's cheek in return. "That is because you are human, and now I see the glory of that. Remember me for me when I have returned to play in the moment."

Phillip's boys, David and James, insisted on helping to carry the baggage out as they had taken it in.

Margaret looked around the crowd. "Have you seen Thomas?"

John looked as well. "No."

They climbed into the wagon and James Duncan snapped the reigns. Everyone waved goodbye and someone started a cheer of "Hip-Hip-Hooray!"

As they rolled through the streets of Glasen, the houses and shops went by and she remembered how they had fascinated her when they first arrived. She regretted that she had not sketched more of them and promised herself that she would return to Nova Scotia and capture the wonderful little towns and the people living in them.

They came to the road leading out to the saw mill. Thomas stepped in front of the wagon from behind a tree and waved his arms. James Duncan pulled up on the reins. "What now?"

Thomas held a piece of paper in one hand. "I had to say goodbye, but I couldn't say it there."

John stood up. "If you and Margaret would like to speak alone..."

"No. I just wanted you both to know that I've applied to the art college. If I'm accepted I'll begin in the spring."

Deep warmth filled Margaret. "Thomas, that's wonderful. If you need help, any kind of help, you know how to reach us. And the moment you have a show, I'll be there."

"Thank you. Thank you for the lessons, and just for everything. You've changed my life, Margaret Talbot. I can never repay you."

She leaned down and gently kissed him on the forehead. "Just be who you are, Thomas. Good luck."

The wagon started on. Thomas quickly handed Margaret a piece of paper. "I almost forgot. This is for you." It was a sketch, much like the one he had done of Ian and Sara going into mass. This time, however, it was John and Margaret at Phillip Lamont's house earlier that day, and it was John's face looking happy after many years of pain and Margaret turning to look at him with a smile so sweet, so loving, it brought tears to her eyes.

Thomas shouted from behind the moving wagon. "I didn't draw it under my tree this time. I don't need that old tree anymore. I'm an artist."

They rounded a corner. Most of the limbs on the trees were bare after being stripped by the storm. Still, some leaves clung on tenaciously. Margaret started to reach for her sketchbook and stopped. The brilliant yellows, fiery oranges, and deep reds shone like sparkling jewels against the dark emerald of the spruce. Then, nearly hidden among the display, she saw that some leaves had not yet changed, their cool green a promise of spring to come.

In her mind the colors splattered across a canvas, the leaves shown as clumps of paint applied thick in a dozen shades that melded one into the other, punctuated with splashes of contrasting color. It was a complete departure from the style she had been trained in, and was like nothing she had ever envisioned before.

Margaret looked to John. He smiled broadly, took her hand and touched it to his cheek. There were still many things to discuss between them, and many hurts to heal. Yet, it was clear that they would heal them, for she now knew who she was and what she truly wanted.

About the Author

David A. Wimsett is a professional writer whose works have appeared in newspapers, magazines and online platforms. He has produced business and technical writing for corporations and universities. Mr. Wimsett is an actor, singer and musician and has appeared as a commentator on television and radio.

He became a single parent in his twenties and both raised and guided his son into adulthood.

He is a member of the Professional Writers Association of Canada and the Canadian Media Guild.

This is his debut novel